Euphoria An Anthology of Thrillers

Vanessa Steele

Published by Trellis Publishing, 2021.

EUPHORIA AN ANTHOLOGY OF THRILLERS

First edition. July 9, 2021.

Copyright © 2021 Vanessa Steele.

ISBN: 979-8224631537

Written by Vanessa Steele.

EUPHORIA

VANESSA STEELE

1

Chapter 1

"Oh!" Elizabeth Bentley exclaimed as soon as she saw that the apples at the local farmer's market had been marked down from their usual price. "Well, this is a lovely surprise." She picked up the reddest apple she could find and bit into it.

Crunch!

"Just as good now as they were during the beginning of the season," said the vendor. "But I think my apples speak for themselves." He handed over a napkin seeing as the juices were running down her chin. "So, how many will it be?"

"I'll take twelve," she answered before taking another bite. "Well, thirteen including this one."

The vendor waved his hand. "That one is on me."

"Are you sure?"

"Absolutely. Things have been slow around here. There's a storm coming in and most people have up and left."

Elizabeth shook her head. "Hurricane or not, I couldn't even think of leaving my home. That's where my husband and I started our lives together. I wouldn't give that up for the world." She smiled fondly as old memories surfaced to the front of her mind. "I still remember the day he carried me over that threshold."

The vendor nodded his understanding and gathered up her order. "Well, I hope you have a wonderful day. And be sure to stay safe during the storm."

"Oh, I will. Our basement was built to withstand this sort of thing so I don't think I have anything to worry about."

"Let's hope so."

Elizabeth took the bag of apples with a brightness to her smile. "I can't wait to get these into the oven."

"Apple pie?" guessed the man.

"Nothing less. It is my husband's favorite. It will be a wonderful surprise for when he gets in this evening."

"Have a good night, then." He waved her off.

In the distance, storm clouds were already starting to gather.

It was going to be a bad one.

***

When Elizabeth arrived at her home, the window shutters were flapping against the side of the house.

"I'll need to close those before the wind gets any worse," she whispered to herself as she approached the front door. She tried the handle and was surprised to find that someone had left it unlocked. "Strange," she said. "I was certain..."

She stepped inside and almost immediately, she could tell that something was off. "Jameson?"

Silence.

"Jameson? Did they send you home early because of the storm?"

Still, there was nothing but silence.

Elizabeth felt her heart pound. Something wasn't right.

She dropped the bag of apples and grabbed a nearby vase. Her hands tightened around the ceramic, preparing herself to use it as a weapon. She prayed it would not come to that but she wasn't about to take any chances.

The old floorboards creaked underfoot. Elizabeth pressed herself against the wall, heart pounding louder than ever. While holding her breath, she waited.

She didn't know what it was that she was waiting for but then, she heard it.

A moan.

It was coming from the bedroom.

As she neared the end of the hall, the moaning was highlighted by a sound that made Elizabeth's blood run cold. She dropped the vase and it shattered against the ground. Before the ceramic could finish scattering into the various corners, Elizabeth had barged through the door. "Jameson!" Her voice sounded odd like it had emerged from the throat of someone else.

Elizabeth blinked, thinking that she was caught in a bad dream. But there he was, tangled together with a younger woman.

For a moment, no one moved. Elizabeth couldn't even remember how to breathe. Her blood had gone from freezing to boiling. By her side, her hands had tightened into fists. "I..." Her mouth burned with the need to speak — to cuss out the man she thought she could trust — but it was like her vocal cords had been snipped by the sight of his infidelity.

"Look, I can explain..." he started as he rose from the bed, brandishing his manhood.

The sight of it was enough to throw Elizabeth into a blind rage. She grabbed the closest object she could find and aimed it at his head.

"Whoa!"

Elizabeth grabbed something else, determined to hit her target this time around. Already, there was an aching in her heart that felt like the stab of a red-hot dagger. If Jameson could make her hurt then she'd return the favor tenfold.

"Get out of my house!" she screamed at the top of her lungs. "Get out! Get out! Get out!" Elizabeth's violence was redirected towards the woman still occupying her bed. She was pretty — a neighbor from down the road that had a certain 'unluckiness' with her car. Every week, it seemed she was back in Jameson's shop, getting it fixed for one problem or another. Elizabeth now understood that it was nothing more than a ploy. She felt betrayed and she would not stand for it.

"Eliza, baby, let's talk about this."

"Talk?" she spat. "There's nothing to talk about. Your crime is as clear as day. And I'll be the judge and jury on this one and say that you're *guilty*."

He grabbed her by the wrist and pulled her close. "I need you to listen to me. This never happened. If word gets out, then my parents will write me off the will."

"Well, you should have thought about that *before* you went off and slept with this tramp!"

The woman gasped with offense at the insult.

"You slept with my *husband*," retorted Elizabeth. "And you knew damn well that he was married when you fell into bed with him so don't play innocent with me."

"You need to calm down." Jameson's grip tightened to the point where he was hurting her. "This cannot get out."

Elizabeth was a Christian woman but at that moment she wanted to scream every swear word in the books. Instead, she rammed her knee into his crotch.

And that's when she made her getaway.

Chapter 2

Elizabeth didn't think about looking back once she started running. She just ran and ran and ran. At some point, her legs began to protest but she did not listen to them. As far as she concerned, she needed to get as far away from her husband as humanly possible. And even then, she wasn't sure whether that would be enough.

Boom!

In the distance, lightning flashed across the landscape. The storm was right on the horizon and if Elizabeth didn't find herself some shelter, she'd be in deep trouble.

She paused by a lamp post and leaned against it in an attempt to catch her breath. In those few moments, the reality slammed into her like a bullet train. Her husband had cheated on her. And she feared that it hadn't been the first time. In all honesty, the couple had probably been seeing each other for weeks. All the while, they had played her for the fool.

Her stomach lurched and she could no longer keep back the rush of emotion. It came out as a pile of sick, half-hidden behind a nearby bush.

"Ma'am, are you alright?" asked a concerned voice. A second later, there was a warm hand laying across the small of her back.

Again, Elizabeth's stomach threatened to escape through her mouth. The stranger pulled back her hair to keep it from getting soiled. Gently, he rubbed circles into her back as if that might help ease the turmoil of her body.

"Do you want me to call a doctor?" he offered.

"No," Elizabeth managed to say as she wiped her mouth with the length of her arm. "I'm fine." She attempted to stand up straight but her legs felt like they had been replaced by a couple of noodles. She swayed forward and saw the world spin before her eyes.

If it hadn't been for the stranger, she would have collapsed onto the ground.

"Easy," he whispered. "I think it might be best for me to call that doctor. You aren't looking too good."

"I'm *fine,*" she insisted. "Now, let me go."

"Under good conscious, I cannot do that. In nothing else, let me bring you down to my hotel."

"Hotel?"

"The Juniper," he explained. "The hotel on Sixth and Saxon."

Elizabeth tried to imagine the building but her mind came up blank. There was just too much for her to deal with for a mental geography jaunt.

Before she could deny his offering, he picked her up and started carrying her down the street. The gesture was meant to help her but instead, it only added to Elizabeth's distress for it reminded her of her wedding day. On that day, she had thought everything perfect. She had thought that it was the beginning of the ideal life — the life she had always dreamed of as a little girl.

Now, all that was ruined.

The tears came silently at first but then they became uncontrollable sobs. She hid her face in the stranger's chest because she could not stand the thought of anyone seeing her in such a vulnerable state.

"Shh, it's okay," he whispered in a soft, soothing voice. "It's okay."

But it was not okay — it was far from okay. All she wanted to do was rewind to yesterday where everything was still as it was supposed to be.

Ding!

As soon as the hotel owner walked through the front door, he was greeted by the familiar sound.

"Sir?"

The girl working the front desk had directed her attention to the entrance at the sound only to find her boss carrying one of the locals. She recognized the woman as the mechanic's wife.

"I need one of our available rooms."

"Uh..."

"Now." The tone of his voice was enough to trigger her into action.

"Right away." She snatched the first key she saw and jogged towards the elevator. The owner was holding open the door with his foot. He had yet to let go of Elizabeth nor did he intend to until they were safely inside one of the hotel rooms. There, he'd find out what troubled her so and he'd make it right because no woman served this kind of sorrow. To leave such a thing unattended...

He couldn't even think of it.

"Um..."

"What is it?" he asked when he saw his worker's hesitation. "I didn't realize the key I had grabbed. If you'd only give me a minute and I'll run down and grab another."

"Nonsense," he answered. "Any room will do."

The girl nibbled her bottom lip, trying to figure out the best way to answer him. "Well, there have been certain complaints about this room..." She fidgeted from foot to foot like she would rather disappear than have the conversation she was having now.

"What kind of complaints?"

She glanced at Elizabeth and did not think it appropriate to share such details in front of a fragile woman.

"I see," said her boss, understanding her lack of response. "Wait here until I return."

Gently, he placed Elizabeth back on her feet. He kept his hand on her shoulder until he was sure that she could stand on her own. Only then did he take the key and open the door, ushering her inside. "I'd like a word," he said as soon as she had eased herself onto the edge of the bed.

"I don't feel much like talking."

"What happened?"

Elizabeth stared past the man, trying not to see the scene that had broken her heart but it was playing itself like a movie, over and over. She still could not understand how Jameson could hurt her in such a manner. After ten years of marriage...

She hung her head in her hands.

"Please," pleaded the man. "I only want to help you."

"Help me?" she scoffed with a shake of her head. "Tell me, what's your name?"

"Dean. Dean Wilson."

"Well, Dean, tell me, have you ever had your heart brutally ripped out of your chest? Have you ever had the one person you could trust stomp all over it without a single thought? Tell me, Dean, how you intend to help me when I'm broken without repair."

"You are not broken," he said as he took her by the shoulders. He waited until she lifted her head to looked at him. Their eyes connected and a spark seemed to fizzle through the air, adding a newfound life pulse to the dull atmosphere. "And you best believe that I am going to do whatever it is that I can to help."

Chapter 3

"Why?"

"Because I know your pain and I have experienced it myself. Five years ago, my wife ran off with my best friend. I haven't heard from them since but every day, I think about what it is that they must be doing and it makes me sick. Most nights, I cannot sleep because I keep trying to rewind the tape and figure out what I did wrong — what I missed along the way because surely, there were clues and had I only paid attention, maybe I wouldn't be alone right now." His voice wavered and Eliza thought that he was on the verge of tears.

But he composed himself with a measured breath.

"And even after all that sleeplessness, I'm no closer to connecting the dots because frankly, there was nothing I could have done to prevent it." He ran his fingers through his hair and turned on his heels, heading for the door. "You are free to stay here for as long as you need. I'll have room service send something up for you."

Outside, Dean found his employee standing where he had left her.

"Sir!" she exclaimed the second she saw him almost like it had been an unexpected surprise.

"Now, what were these complaints you were telling me about?"

"Right." She wrung her fingers together.

Dean was starting to lose his patience.

"A few of our guests have described weird occurrences in that room. Most of them have requested a different room within a couple of hours. And the story is always the same — there's someone in the mirror."

"The mirror?"

"Yes. They say that it is a woman and that she likes to talk..."

"This is nonsense," said Dean. "And I am not fond of such practical jokes."

"It is not a practical joke!"

"Have you seen this woman yourself?"

"Well, no, I haven't."

"And yet, you believe that she is real?"

"I believe that something isn't right with that room," she said. "Because I get goosebumps every time I go in there."

"Nothing more than a draft," he dismissed. "Now, I will have no more talk of ghosts. Do I make myself clear?"

She glanced at the door with a look of apprehension. "Crystal."

"Good. Now, I want you to open a tab for that young woman and place it under my name. From this point forward, she is my personal guest."

***

Elizabeth heard a knock on the door and thought about ignoring it. She wasn't hungry anyway. In fact, there was a possibility that she would never regain her appetite.

Knock! Knock!

There was a slight pause before the doorknob started to turn.

In came Dean with a tray of food. "Oh, good, you're still here. I had begun to worry that you had left when you failed to answer the door."

"Where would I go?" she asked. "When my husband is with another woman in the place I had once called my home."

Dean placed the food on the small table by the fireplace and once again joined Elizabeth on the edge of the bed. Gently, he laid his hand on her knee and gave it a slight squeeze. "You cannot let this incident ruin your life."

Elizabeth looked away and through the window. It was dark and she could hear the distant thundering that accompanied the storm.

"As far as I'm concerned, that husband of yours was nothing more than a fool for cheating on such a beautiful woman."

Her cheeks flushed with a bright crimson color.

"Please, eat something. And if there is anything that you need, do not hesitate to find me."

Elizabeth nodded. "Thank you. I appreciate everything that you have done for me thus far. It is not common to find someone so generous of heart."

"As I said, I am familiar with your pain and only wish to ease it from your soul because I know how unbearable it can be to have that kind of weight pressing down on your heart."

And he was right. It was like a vice squeezing around her heart, tighter and tighter.

"Please..." she whispered. "I need some time to think."

"Of course," he said with a nod. "But remember what I said. If you need anything — anything at all — come and find me."

"I will."

Elizabeth waited for him to leave. She even waited until his footsteps grew silent. Only then did she rise to her feet. The food was steaming with various aromas but none of them worked to awaken her appetite. She turned her head and covered her mouth with her hand to prevent herself from getting sick.

Needing the fresh air, she opened the window and stuck her head outside. She gulped in breath after breath like a woman resurfaced. Her lungs expanded and her mind seemed to become clearer.

"Perhaps he is right. I shouldn't let Jameson be the ruin of my life when it is obvious that I mean little to him." With this thought, she turned around, determined to eat something.

And that's when she saw the shadow. At first, she thought it a figment of her imagination but the more she stared at it, the more definition it gained.

"Who are you?" she demanded of the shadow. "And what are you doing in my room."

"I'm here to help you," responded the shadow with a voice like silk. "Only come closer and I will tell you everything that you need to know."

Chapter 4

Elizabeth knew that it was crazy for her to talk to a shadow lurking inside a hotel mirror but for some reason, she found herself inching forward like she was being drawn in by some invisible force.

"Who are you?"

"I am you," answered the shadow. "I am a woman cheated."

Elizabeth was close enough to touch the mirror but she could bring herself to do it.

"And I know things about that husband of yours..." crackled the voice.

"I have lost my mind to heightened stress," thought Elizabeth. *"That is the only explanation for this madness."*

"This is not madness," said the shadow as if it were capable of reading Elizabeth's mind.

"But you are nothing more than a shadow..."

"I am you," repeated the specter. "A woman cheated."

Elizabeth shook her head as if that might erase the craziness of the moment but to her dismay, the shadow remained. More than ever, its features were clearer than ever. Elizabeth could see that the shadow was a middle-aged woman with bright blue eyes and hair as wild as a bird's nest. "Did you find your husband sleeping with a younger woman."

"You might think that that woman is your husband's only lover but she is but one on a long list."

"No..."

"Indeed. Your husband has bedded half the town. Do you not think it peculiar that half his clientele consists of young, single females."

"I never thought about it..." Elizabeth had to hold on to the edge of the dresser to keep herself from collapse. Every word spoken by the shadow felt like a dagger straight through her heart. "How could I have been so blind?"

"Love cripples us," said the shadow. "It makes us vulnerable to the crimes of men."

Boom!

The lights in the hotel flickered as a violent gust of wind whipped against the side of the building. The rain came down in buckets, pelting the window panes.

Boom!

There came another crash of thunder, much louder this time. It shook the very floor she was standing on. The silverware on her dinner tray rattled with the force of it.

Elizabeth stood as still as a statue, waiting for another but it never came. She turned around, ready to resume her conversation with the shadow but she was no longer there. "Hello?" she whispered aloud. She felt silly for doing so for clearly, she was the only one in the room.

"I need a drink," she thought. *"Badly."*

***

She found Dean at the bar with a drink of his own. He had it cradled against his hands like a precious object. He was staring deep into that amber liquid like it might reveal some token of valuable information.

Elizabeth took a seat beside the man.

He looked up and the corners of his lips twitched into a half-smile. "Ah, Elizabeth."

"I'll have a sherry."

"Feeling better?" he asked, turning in her direction. "Or have you come to drown away your sorrows?"

"A bit of both," she answered. "But more than anything, the storm was starting to get to me. I feared it would come crashing through my window at any moment. I feel much safer down here." Elizabeth didn't bother to tell him about the woman in the mirror because she did not want to come across as a crazy woman. Besides, it had only been a figment of her imagination.

"Did you manage to eat anything?"

"I'm not hungry."

"You have to eat," insisted Dean. "I know that your stomach is probably tied up in a knot but you still have to eat."

"I can't."

"Will you at least try?"

"Fine."

"Wait here. I will get you something from the kitchen."

Elizabeth took the moment of solitude to chug down most of her wine. The warmth of it helped to calm her nerves. Of course, she hadn't seen a shadow in the mirror. That would be nothing short of insanity.

Still, she could not stop thinking about that shadow and everything it had spoken to her. Perhaps...

"No," she said aloud.

"Excuse me?" quipped the bartender.

"Nothing."

He shrugged and disappeared into the back, dirty dishes in hand.

Elizabeth watched him go but out of the corner of her eye, she noticed a wisp of darkness. She turned her head ever so slowly. "It's you," she whispered. "No. But it can't be. You're not real."

"Oh, but I am. You can deny me all you'd like but that will not change a thing."

"No. No. No. No. No." Elizabeth repeated the word over and over again. "I can't be losing my mind."

"If you ask me, you're perfectly sane."

Elizabeth dared to open her eyes. "Sane people do not speak to shadows."

"Maybe so but I am not a shadow. I am you. A woman cheated."

"Stop saying that!" Elizabeth grabbed her glass of wine and threw it at the mirror lining the bar. It shattered, spiderwebbing in every direction.

Silence followed the destruction.

"Did you think that would be enough?" The voice had returned, multiple one hundred fold. "I am here to help you and until I accomplish my task, this is nothing you can do to get rid of me."

"And how are you going to help me?"

"I'm going to tell you what it is that you need to do."

Again, Elizabeth felt herself being drawn in by the voice. It had this sweetness to it that was hard to ignore.

"That husband of yours needs to pay for his crimes. He injured you, did he not?"

Elizabeth found herself nodding.

"Then I think that it's only fair that you injure him, too."

"Injure him?"

"Put him out of his misery for dogs like that do not deserve to live."

"Wait..." Elizabeth furrowed her brows together, slowly connecting the dots. "Are you suggesting that I *kill* my husband?"

"It is a desire deep inside your heart. All you need to do is listen."

And it was true. Her heart seemed to beat with the new tune of *kill, kill, kill.*

"I want to kill my husband..." she said in a voice that did not sound like her own.

"You want to kill your husband."

Chapter 5

Dean returned from the kitchen to find the bartender looking rather pale. "What's going on? Where did Elizabeth go?"

"She rushed me and demanded the biggest knife we had," answered the young man. "I didn't know what to do so I gave her the knife..."

Dean cursed under his breath. "In what direction did she go?"

The bartender managed to point toward the south exit. "Sir, she looked awfully deranged."

"Let me handle this but if I do not return in an hour's time, I want you to call the police."

"The police?"

But Dean didn't both to clarify his directions to the boys because he was already running. There wasn't a single second to spare. He wasn't about to let Elizabeth ruin her own life. He had to stop her before she could do the unthinkable.

Outside, the heavens had opened, unleashing hell on earth. Trees had fallen over and power lines swayed with the wind. Roof shingles littered the ground.

Dean tried to protect his face with the length of his arm but the rain felt like needles pricking against both his cheeks. He blinked against the torrent of water but the landscape remained blurry. He was never going to find her in this mess.

"Elizabeth!" he shouted but the only response he received was the howling of the wind. "Elizabeth!"

His clothes were soaked through but he did not think about turning back. He kept on shouting until his throat was red and raw and even then, he continued to call out her name.

A few feet away, lightning struck a tree. The wood splintered and smoldered. Dean got to taste some of it against his skin. He picked out most of it from his arm. The blood was washed away by the rain.

He stopped to catch his breath and that's when he saw her. She was just standing there, knife in hand. In front of her was a quaint little house, complete with flower boxes in every window. Elizabeth had taken every care in the world to paint those flower boxes, wanting her home to be the best looking one in the entire neighborhood. She had wanted her husband to feel proud about coming home from work each and every day. It occurred to her now that her efforts had been pointless. Jameson did not care about the flower boxes. All he had cared about was finding his next conquest.

"Elizabeth."

She did not hear the hotel owner, even as he approached her.

"Elizabeth," he said a second time.

In a flash of movement, she whipped around, branding her knife. "What are you doing here?"

"Elizabeth, put down the knife."

Inside of listening, she tightened her fingers around the handle. "No. My husband deserves this."

"No one deserves to die," countered Dean. "Even the worst criminals on this planet deserve the right to live."

"No!"

Dean held out both his hands to show that he wasn't a threat. "I need you to listen to me."

"No, I need you to listen to me." She charged forward and pressed the tip of the knife against the side of his neck. "The shadow told me to do it."

"The shadow?" Dean was holding himself extremely still for he feared if he did anything abrupt, Elizabeth would in fact slice his neck open.

"From the hotel." Elizabeth wavered for a moment. "It was a woman with blue eyes..."

"And what did this woman tell you?"

"That she was I, a cheated woman."

"Okay. And she was the one who told you to kill your husband?"

Elizabeth nodded. "She told me that it was a desire inside my heart and I listened." Her arm dropped and with it, the knife. "And I do want to kill him, I do!"

"I know." Dean wrapped her in his arms before she could do anything drastic. "But I need you to listen to me now. That shadow in the hotel mirror does not exist. Your mind was only playing tricks on you."

"But she was so real..."

"I know."

"And her voice so convincing."

He gently lifted her head by the chin so that she was forced to look at him. "Can you not see that this is preposterous?"

"I don't know what to think anymore..."

Dean kissed the top of her head. "Come on, we are going to catch a cold if we remain exposed to this rain."

***

And so, Dean brought her back to his hotel and straight to his private room. "Let me draw you a warm bath. It'll help calm you down."

Elizabeth didn't say a word. Determined to get to the bottom of this shadow business, she walked up to the mirror and tapped on the glass. "Hello?"

There was no response.

She tapped on it again, hoping to awaken the woman living on the other side.

Dean watched from the doorway, a frown on his face. Elizabeth was broken. He could see the fractures of her soul written all over her face. Desperately, he wanted to mend them — to put her back together again — but only time would heal those wounds.

"She wasn't real..."

"In the way, she was the hatred inside your heart. But you must never listen to that hatred or else it will destroy you."

Elizabeth fell to her knees. "I was going to kill my husband..."

"But you didn't."

"I was going to slice his throat with a knife..."

Dean ran his fingers through her hair. "Shh, it'll be okay. It'll be hard but this too shall pass." And with that, he helped her into the bathroom where she soaked against the hot water, letting it melt away all the troubles that ailed her.

Epilogue

Two years later.

Elizabeth walked along the farmer's market, looking for fresh apples to take home with her. She had yet to find the vendor she had been searching for.

Along the water, she came across a trinket shop. The woman sitting towards the back looked oddly familiar. The blue of her eyes was enough to send a shiver done her spine.

"Hello," said the woman. "Are you looking for anything in particular?"

"N-No," she stammercd.

"Perhaps I could interest you in something from our clearance." The woman smiled, showing off teeth that seemed far too white for her age. "Like this lovely hand mirror carved from an elephant tusk."

Elizabeth took the mirror and turned it slowly so that she could admire her reflection. Somehow, she seemed younger. Her wrinkles were less defined and her skin held a certain glow to it.

"A pretty girl like you needs a mirror like this one. For you, I'll offer quite the deal — one that's impossible to walk away from."

Elizabeth blinked and all of a sudden, the edges of the mirror were outlined in black.

"No..." she whispered underneath her breath. The shadow began to creep from the background, getting closer and closer to her reflection. Elizabeth could feel it starting to breathe down her neck.

"There you are." Dean's familiar voice broke her from her trance. "I've been looking everywhere for you."

"Sorry," she mumbled before looking back at the mirror. The shadow was gone. Once again, Dean had saved her from the darkness in her mind. After all these years, he was still the only person who could keep her sane. Without him, she would have ended up at an asylum sooner rather than later.

"Have you found anything?"

"No." Elizabeth returned the mirror to its table and walked away. She wasn't going to let that part of her life creep up on her and ruin everything she had worked for.

Dean took her hand and laced their fingers together. "I think I found that apple vendor you were telling me about."

So, Elizabeth followed him through the maze of booths.

After a few short minutes, Elizabeth was faced with a familiar smile. "Ah," said the man. "More apple pie?"

"More apple pie," she confirmed.

He chuckled and bagged up a dozen apples and handed them over. "They're on the house."

Elizabeth shook her head. "I cannot accept that. You worked hard to grow these apples. Please, let me pay for them."

"I insist," he said, winking in Dean's direction.

***

"Why did the apple vendor wink at you?" asked Elizabeth once she was inside the hotel's kitchen. Since it was the off-season and lunch had already been served, the place was deserted.

"I don't know what you're talking about."

Elizabeth stopped and placed a hand on her hip. "Do not lie to me. I saw him wink."

Dean shrugged. "If he did, I didn't see it."

She narrowed her eyes with suspicion. "You are up to something and I do not like it."

Dean did not bother to respond. Instead, he made himself busy by gathering up the materials she needed. Apple pie had quickly become his favorite dessert and Elizabeth was more than happy to make it for him. At times, it was even offered as a special on the hotel menu.

"Oh, this came for you in the mail." Dean dropped a large manilla envelope on the counter.

"Where did this come from?"

"The mailbox."

She clicked her tongue against the roof of her mouth, something she did only in the throes of irritation. If Dean intended to sour her mood, he was certainly on the right path to getting there.

Nevertheless, she opened the envelope. "Is this...?"

"I believe they are."

Elizabeth could not believe her eyes. It was the divorce papers she had been waiting for. Finally, she was free of the monster that had broken her heart. At the bottom was Jameson's signature, officially sealing the deal that they were no longer man and wife. For the first time, Elizabeth was able to breathe properly. That tightness around her chest ceased to exist.

"I can't believe it..." she whispered as she read over the words.

When she finally lifted her eyes from the documents, Dean had disappeared. She frowned, wondering where he had run off to. But then she looked down and saw him kneeling. In his hand was a little black box. The diamond ring it housed was the most beautiful thing that Elizabeth had ever laid her eyes on. The way it glimmered reminded her of the nighttime sky and all of its glorious twinkling stars.

"Eliza, will you marry me?" Dean did not mince words because there was only one thing that he wanted and that was to start a new life with this woman. They had both been cheated and broken but together he was confident that they something special — something that could last an eternity.

"Yes!" she exclaimed as she ran forward and smothered him against her arms. "A thousand times, yes!" She wanted to scream from the rooftops but it felt surreal that she would be given a second chance at love.

He pulled her close and their lips collided into a passion-filled kiss.

Her breath was taken away by the feeling of pure euphoria. Even with Jameson, she had never felt this way. Perhaps she had only fooled herself into thinking that she loved the man she now called her ex-husband. Because this — this was real.

"Eliza..." he whispered as he held both her cheeks in his hands. "There is something I must ask of you before I put this ring on your finger."

"What?"

"Promise me that you won't try to kill me with a knife."

"Promise me that you won't cheat on me and you'll never have that problem," she countered.

"I promise."

"Then, like I said, you have nothing to worry about."

END

HORROR ETERNAL

25

JESSICA BARKER

Another dead end. Clarissa shuffled down the dark alley. Her feet were dragging, and she was absentmindedly scratching again. The track marks of her nails lined her arms and neck. The hunger was an itch she couldn't scratch. It made her skin crawl. She was reduced to being a junkie, always searching for her next fix, always hoping for a cure. This was her life now. Someone else's stupid mistake had ripped away everything that she loved. The worst part was that now she understood the hunger that compelled her attacker, and now that same need had her by the throat.

Clarissa squeezed her eyes shut as dingy yellow headlights swept passed her. She was more sensitive to light now. Her eyes functioned better at night, better for hunting. The car rumbled at the end of the alley. Rain drops shone like liquid confetti in the beams from the headlights.

The front passenger window rolled down. "Get in." A man dressed in a dark shirt peered out at her.

Meals on wheels. At least her sarcasm was still intact. Clarissa reached out her hand and opened the door. The tremors in her hands were getting worse. She needed to feed soon. The nausea and dry heaving would start next. The man switched gears and sped down the road. Streetlights in disrepair stood darkly by the roadside, sad reminders of their previous purpose.

His heartbeat was a haunting melody. *Thump, thump.* A solitary drum beating out the song of life. *Thump, thump.* The mouthwatering pounding of something alive. *Thump, thump.* Clarissa couldn't take it anymore. She bared her fangs and lunged at the driver.

The palm of his hand landed squarely on her forehead, pushing her back. Without taking his eyes off the road, he tutted at her like she was a misbehaving dog. "Unh uh!" Weak with hunger, Clarissa tried to push past him, but it was no use. He flicked her in the middle of her forehead. "Look in the glovebox."

Her frustrated fingers clawed at the lever on the glovebox until it opened. Inside in all its crimson glory was a pouch of blood. Clarissa almost cried with joy as she fumbled the pouch out of the cubbyhole. The man cleared his throat and pointed to the green crazy straw that had been under the pouch. Clarissa scrambled to grab the straw and pierced the thin plastic of the bag.

"Think of it as the vampire version of Capri Sun." The man smirked as she slurped down the thick, tangy liquid. It had a meaty, copper taste that washed over her tongue. The blood took the edge off. Her tremors stopped almost immediately.

"Who are you?" Clarissa managed to say the words around the straw in her mouth.

"For now, let's just say we have a mutual acquaintance." The car turned down a side street.

Dirty buildings caked in years of soot and grime loomed on either side of the car. Rats scurried down into the grates on the side of the road. The once proud neighborhood was now a forlorn crone. Her vision was plagued with fogged up cataract windows and cobwebs of time. Bent street signs curled the wicked fingers of their metal frames, beckoning the car forward.

The man parked outside of a brick building. The settling of the building's foundations had wrenched cracks through its exterior. A single yellow light bulb glowed naked over the door. "Come on. He's expecting you." The man killed the engine and climbed out of the car. As he walked, Clarissa noticed a slight limp in his gait.

"Who is expecting me?" She followed him uneasily towards the entrance.

The man didn't answer. He jiggled a worn key into the lock and rammed it with his shoulder. The warped foundation and years of summer heat had twisted the doorframe so that it no longer allowed the door to move easily. The man went inside. He eyed the young woman still standing on the stoop and raised his eyebrow as if to hurry her up.

"Well, what are you waiting for? Come in." Impatience rolled off of his tongue.

Clarissa stepped inside slowly. Spiders figure skated between balusters on the staircase, weaving intricate lace patterns with their webs. The man shoved the door shut behind them and walked to a room on the right. Peeling wooden doors were pulled apart enough for a person to slip through. Clarissa scanned the shadows for potential threats. Without saying anything, the man who had driven her vanished into the room on the other side of the doors. Taking a deep breath, she followed him.

A man with curly blonde hair was sitting in front of a fireplace. Books lined the far wall. A tumbler of thick, red liquid sloshed in his hand. "You!" Clarissa's eyes turned to daggers as she recognized him. The scene from the night she was attacked played in her head.

She had been ending her shift at Momma's Café. The tiny bell over the door tinkled lightly. Clarissa had been wiping down the counter. "We're closed."

"I'm hungry."

Clarissa glanced behind her to see a curly blonde-haired man with blue eyes. "The cook has already gone home." She paused. He looked so tired. "I can get you a piece of pie if you like."

The soft click of the front door locking sent a chill down her spine. The man had a twisted smile on his face. "I was thinking of something with a little more kick."

He lunged at her. Clarissa screamed and tried to jump over the counter, but the man grabbed her wrist and then her waist. Her feet flailed wildly, trying to kick her way free. Her cries faded to pleading. "No, please! Let me go!"

"Shhh. It will only hurt for a second." His words hissed in her ear.

As she whimpered, something stabbed her neck. The pain was instant and sharp, but soon it ebbed away. The pain was replaced with a numbing sensation. She felt something warm wash over her. Her eyes fluttered. The world was getting darker and blurry. Clarissa fought to stay conscious, but it was no use. Sleep was calling to her. All she had to do was slip away, then everything would be over.

When she had woken up a few hours later, her mouth had something crusty and red smeared over it. Her senses seemed raw. At the time, she had chalked it up to trauma and adrenaline. Somehow, she had managed to stumble home. Clarissa's body had shivered, and she had spent the rest of the night dry heaving. Little did she know, that was only the beginning.

"You're the one who attacked me! You're the reason I'm like this!" Clarissa lunged at him. Anger flared in her eyes. Her nails reached out like tiny, half-moon daggers.

The dark-haired man who had driven her there stepped between Clarissa and the other man. He grabbed her arm and pinned it behind her back. The blonde waved his hand. "Cyrus, that's enough. She's upset and understandably so. Clarissa has had quite the life change lately."

"Quite the life change?! That's what you call this? You turned me into a vampire!" She jerked her arm away from Cyrus's grasp.

"Would you like to know why I chose you?" The blonde sipped from his tumbler.

Scoffing, Clarissa threw her hands up in the air. "Sure. Tell me why you chose to make me a monster. What made me so special that you had to take away my humanity?"

"Your hair."

"My hair?"

"When I stepped into the café that night, I was out of my mind with hunger. Your hair, your beautiful auburn hair, looked like dried blood in the lighting. It was the same color of my mother's hair. That is the only reason you are alive right now. You should consider yourself lucky."

"Lucky?!" Clarissa cried out, but the blonde's ears seemed to pick up on something.

"What is it, Uther?" Cyrus slipped his hand to the waistband of his pants where a pistol was tucked.

A loud bang followed by splintering wood resounded near the front door. "Get her out of here!" Uther was on his feet in an instant. His eyes scanned the room.

As Cyrus grabbed Clarissa's wrist, she heard a woman's voice call out to them playfully. "Come out, come out, wherever you are."

"Quickly!" Uther yelled out to get them moving.

Cyrus pulled a book on a shelf, and a hidden passage appeared. More crashing sounds echoed behind them. He pulled Clarissa along in his wake. Glancing over her shoulder before the passage closed, Clarissa saw a woman clad in all black tossing a wooden stake back and forth between her hands. The woman and Uther circled one another menacingly. Before she could see anything else, the crack in the passage's entrance sealed itself shut. Cyrus was pulling her at a full run now. The faster he ran, the faster his heartbeat was. The pounding in his veins called out to her. Clarissa felt her fangs start to drip with the numbing toxin that always subdued her prey.

The passage ended abruptly. "Now what?!" She tried to catch her breath and distract herself from the rhythm of the blood flowing through him.

"We climb." He pointed up to a rusty ladder hanging above their heads.

"What? I'm not climbing that thing. Look at it! Who was that woman? Why did we have to leave like that?" Questions tumbled out of her mind, but the one question she was dying to know the answer to remained unasked in the back of her mind: How would Cyrus's blood taste?

While she played out scenarios in her head of ways to take him by surprise, Cyrus glared at her with hatred in his brown eyes. "That woman was Victoria Miles. She kills vampires for sport. Not because she thinks she is saving people. Not because she thinks it is for the greater good. She does it because she likes the way it makes her feel. So, if you don't want to climb, then be my guest. You can wait for her here. I on the other hand don't intend to let Uther's sacrifice go to waste." Cyrus jumped up and grabbed one of the rungs with his hands. Pulling himself up, he began to climb the ladder. His movements dislodged the pistol from his pants. He cursed under his breath as it toppled to the ground.

The gravity of the situation punched Clarissa in the gut. Uther had stayed behind to give them enough time to get away. He may have saved her this time, but that didn't cancel out the fact that he was the reason she was this way. Now, a psycho vampire hunter was on their tail. A loud crash echoed from the entrance to the passage. The walls shook, and loose debris rained down from the ceiling. Clarissa had no intention of being her next victim. She jumped up, and her fingertips grazed the bottom rung. It wasn't good enough. She had to jump higher. Bracing herself, she leapt again. This time her fingers hooked around the metal bar. Her feet swung freely under her. A light whistling tune echoed down the tunnel. Victoria was coming. Clarissa was running out of time.

She looked up, and Cyrus was already hoisting his body out for the top of the shaft. In sudden, jerking motions, Clarissa managed somehow to pull herself up the ladder until her feet could reach the lowest rung. The whistling was getting louder now. She had never known that such a happy tune could cause so much terror in her. Climbing as fast as she could, Clarissa fumbled her way up the shaft.

Cyrus was waiting at the top to pull her out. As she looked around, Clarissa noticed they were on the roof of a neighboring building. He slid a metal trap door at their feet shut and placed a bar across it to secure it in place. Clarissa noticed a slightly lighter blue fading into the night sky on the horizon. It was almost dawn.

"Ready?" Cyrus planted his left foot in front of his right and bounced on the balls of his feet.

"Ready for what?"

Taking a running start, Cyrus leapt from the edge of the building. His body arched through the air. Landing with a muffled groan, Cyrus stood up and dusted himself off. The trap door next to Clarissa rattled. Gunshots echoed from below. Bullets ripped through the metal barrier. Victoria had found Cyrus's gun. *You've got to be kidding me.* Clarissa took a deep breath and ran. A frightened scream echoed from her throat. The alley below her gaped open like the maw of a giant beast waiting to swallow her whole.

The toe of her sneaker teetered on the edge of the building where Cyrus had landed. Her stomach bottomed out. Clarissa could feel her body beginning to topple backwards. Her arms windmilled in the blank space around her. There was nothing to grab. Would a fall from this high up kill a vampire?

As she fell backwards, something grabbed the waistband of her pants. Cyrus anchored his heels on the roof and hauled her back towards him. Clarissa's arms clung to him. She tried to swallow her heart which was trying to fly out of her mouth. Maybe he was better alive than as a snack pack. She was starting to see why Uther had kept him around.

"Thanks."

"Thank me later." Cyrus pried her hands off of him and jogged to a fire escape that was draped over the edge of the building.

The two of them clanged down the metal steps. The sky was getting lighter with each passing second. Her skin was starting to ache as if she had a dull sunburn. Each movement made her clothing rake against her raw skin. Cyrus banged his fist on a reinforced door. A camera overhead in the alley turned to get a better look at them. An internal mechanism slid open. Cyrus yanked the door open and shoved her inside.

Clarissa looked around the room he had pushed her into. It was small. Only big enough for a few people. The other side of the room had a larger door and what she assumed was a one-way mirror. Cyrus shut the door to the alley behind them.

A voice crackled over a speaker. "Well, well, well, Cyrus, what are you doing here without Uther? You know not all of us agree with the arrangement you two have."

"Uther is dead." Cyrus held his head up.

"Dead?" The voice sounded surprised.

"Victoria Miles finally got him."

Hissing echoed over the speakers. "Did you lead her here?!"

"No. She didn't see where we went."

"You know that with Uther out of the picture, we have no reason to keep you alive." Gas started to hiss through tiny vents overhead.

Cyrus started to choke. He dropped to his knees. Clarissa looked from where he was clutching at his throat to the mirror. "Stop it! You're killing him!"

"You're not human." It was a statement, not a question.

"Yeah! That's right. I'm not human. And if you don't stop whatever the hell is killing him, then I swear I will murder each and every one of you!" She opened her mouth to show her fangs.

Laughter chimed over the speakers, but the gas stopped. Cyrus coughed and gasped for air. The door at the other end of the room unlocked. Clarissa helped Cyrus to his feet. The two of them walked slowly through the door. The inside resembled a speakeasy bar. A man in a suit was chuckling.

"Did you hear that? The big, bad vampire is going to kill us all." He took a sip from a flask. A dark-skinned woman snorted from behind the bar.

Clarissa held her head up higher. "I don't see why you find that so funny."

"It's funny because to me you are little more than a mayfly. You still have the cocky demeanor of a babe who thinks it is invincible. It's clear by the dark circles under your eyes and the fresh scratches that you haven't learned to control your cravings. I'm more curious how you ended up with her." He turned to look at Cyrus. "Did my brother finally break down and make a protégé?"

"Uther wanted to teach her how to live, but Victoria got to him first. It was his final wish for me to save her."

"Well," the man turned to Clarissa, "I suppose that would make me your uncle of sorts. I owe my brother many things. I think assisting his charge with her transformation will suffice to even our debts."

"If he was your brother, then why aren't you upset that he's most likely dead?" Clarissa couldn't stop herself.

"Uther and I have been dead for quite a while. If anything, he is now free. There is no need to mourn him." He took another swig from his flask. "It's almost dawn. The first rule to being a well-adjusted vampire is plenty of rest and plenty of fluids." He tossed her a second flask he had tucked in an inside pocket in his suit jacket. "Cyrus, show her to my brother's old room, will you? I think it is fitting."

Clarissa clutched the flask to her chest. She followed Cyrus down a corridor to large room with a big bed. Golden artifacts were scattered in chests around the room. "What is this place? Why did that guy try to kill you?"

Cyrus sighed and leaned against the bedroom door. "This is where vampires come to feed in peace. Emrick runs the place. He and Uther didn't always see eye to eye on how their kind should live."

"What did he mean? The arrangement you had? What was that about?"

"Uther found me when I was a baby. My mom was dying from a drug overdose in an alley. Some vampires had attacked her while she was OD'ing. They didn't care that I was there or that they were killing her in front of me. If he hadn't gotten there when he did, they probably would have gotten me, too. He saved me and raised me. Emrick and some of the other vampires didn't exactly agree with his choice."

"I'm so sorry."

Cyrus shook his head. "I'm not telling you this for your sympathy. I'm telling you so that you know the man who turned you wasn't all bad."

She still held a grudge, but something was nagging at her. "So, you've been around vampires your whole life?"

"Pretty much."

"Have you...have you heard anything about a cure?" Clarissa couldn't help the trace of hope bubbling up inside of her. She had spent almost every night since she was turned trying to find some way back to her humanity. She had been coming back from another attempt to find anything that might lead her to a cure when Cyrus had pulled up into the alley earlier.

He chuckled and shook his head. "When I was young, I used to read everything I could get my hands on trying to find a cure for Uther. He became like a father to me, and I wanted what any little boy wanted: a normal family. Stop wasting your time, Clarissa. This is who you are now."

"Where are you going?" She felt a slight panic as he started to leave. It was silly, but he was the only one she knew here.

"I need a drink. You'll be safe here. Get some sleep."

For the first time, she noticed the tired sadness in his eyes. Clarissa had been so wrapped up in her own issues she hadn't stopped to think about anyone else. Uther may have just been some vampire that changed her, but to Cyrus he was like family. The sudden loss must have been hitting him harder than he was letting on.

Her head sank to the pillow. She could smell him. Uther. His scent was on the pillows and blankets. She held up the flask Emrick had given her in a small tribute to the dead before drinking from it. As the blood touched her lips, she looked up at the canopy above her bed—Uther's bed.

Gold and silver threads embroidered the red fabric above her. Clarissa tilted her head to the side. There was something familiar about the branching design. She couldn't quite put her finger on it. In the center was an ornate picture of a tree. It seemed to be the anchor point from which all of the other threads radiated out in a series of straight lines. While she stared up at the designs trying to figure out what they reminded her of, her eyelids drooped shut.

Mossy rocks plummeted down towards the rushing sea below. Clarissa could taste the salt on her lips. The vegetation was lush and rich green in color. She felt someone behind her and turned around. Uther's curly blonde hair waved in the ocean breeze.

"This was one of my favorite places on the coast of Wales. Lyssa, Emrick, and I grew up here." He breathed in the cool air.

"You're dead. That woman attacked you." Clarissa shook her head. She must be dreaming.

"Part of me will live on in you. I'm sorry I'm not there to help you through this. Trust Cyrus. He's been with me long enough to know more about the world of vampires than any human should." Uther began to fade. She could see the countryside through his body. "There is something though that I never shared with him."

"What is it?" His voice was becoming fainter.

"Take care of him for me."

"What didn't you share with him? Is it about a cure?!"

"Not all maps are black and white." Uther's outline shimmered in the air before he was completely gone. On the breeze, a cheery tune drifted towards her. The melody stung her ears. In the dream, she thought she recognized it as the same song she had heard being whistled down the tunnel.

Clarissa woke up in a cold sweat. The strange surroundings made her do a double take. Pressing a hand to her racing heart, she looked up.

The embroidery tugged at her mind. What had Uther said? Something about a map? Clarissa stared at the pattern. Suddenly she recognized what was so familiar about it. The golden branches lined up with the layout of the streets and alleys she knew so well. The silver threads seemed to be something different. Maybe something on a different level? What was the tree supposed to signify? Could this finally be a clue to help her find the cure she had been searching for? If there was a cure and Uther knew about it, why wouldn't he have taken it? She found it hard to believe that Uther would show up in her dreams talking about maps at this exact moment if she wasn't supposed to do something.

Wiggling out of the cocoon of blankets, she stood up on the bed and looked at one corner of the canopy. A loose thread dangled down. Clarissa tugged on it. A small rip started at the corner. Jerking the fabric, she managed to rip the embroidered canopy away from the posts. It tore a little around the edges, but for the most part it stayed intact.

Clarissa stumbled off of the bed. Was it dark outside yet? There weren't any clocks in the room. She had no way of knowing how long she had slept. If it was still daylight, she couldn't leave. Her eyes landed on a rug that was wrinkled at one corner. With everything so pristine in the room, the rumpled carpeting stood out.

The room seemed to get colder as she approached it. Clarissa held out one hand to check for a draft along the walls. Hidden doors in walls seemed like something a vampire who owned a speakeasy would incorporate into his building. The cold breeze tickled the bottom of her palm, but it wasn't coming from the walls. She followed the air current to a section in the floor.

Pulling back the rug, Clarissa saw a large metal ring set into the flooring. She pulled on the ring. Groaning from years of not being used, a section of the floor came up like a hatch. Clarissa peered into the dark space under the flooring. Her keen eyes could make out a tunnel about eight feet down. A sudden rush of air stung her cheeks.

Butterflies flitted in her stomach with nervous excitement. Taking a moment to steel her nerves, Clarissa sat on the edge of the opening with her feet dangling into the darkness. It looked light tight. Even if the sun was still out, she would be protected if she was underground. Clarissa pushed herself off the edge and allowed her body to drop. The canopy was still clutched in her hand. The tunnel was dry and smooth. It seemed time had worn away any rough edges. The chill of the underground prickled her skin. Her fingers found the silver thread she was pretty certain would match up with her location. Clarissa slowly moved forward, following the path the embroidery seemed to line out.

Squeaking above her drew her attention. Tiny bats squirmed overhead. Her footsteps were disturbing their sleep. Clarissa tried to quiet her movements. She could see something further down the tunnel. It was recessed into a stone archway. The tunnel became silent as she approached the large, stone door. The soundless void made her ears ache. It was like the calm before a storm. The bats that were restless only seconds before didn't even dare to breathe now.

Clarissa stood in front of the door. "Great. No knob. Now what?" Her eyes settled on two indentions in the wall. Dark brown smudges stained the stone. Clarissa leaned in and sniffed the stains. Blood. She raised one finger to her mouth and pricked the tip on one of her fangs. Fresh blood bubbled from the tiny nick. "Here goes nothing." Her trembling finger pressed to both grooves leaving behind a smear of red.

The stone rumbled and scraped against the top and bottom of the tunnel. Clarissa's heart pounded against her ribcage. She tried to prepare herself for whatever was behind the door as it slid away. The embroidered fabric slipped out of her hand to the floor of the tunnel. The first thing she noticed was the smell.

The room was musty. Undertones of death wafted towards her. Clarissa wrinkled her nose and took a tentative step forward. In the center of the room was a pedestal. A wooden box was perched atop it. Carvings down the side of the pedestal showed leaves at the top followed by a tree trunk and roots. Doors similar to the one she came through lined the circular wall around the room.

Clarissa moved towards the pedestal. Her fingertips traced the edges of the box. Could this be it? The cure? Her hopes fluttered up into her throat. Lifting the lid, she held her breath. Once the box was open, it began to play a melody. The notes sent chills down her spine. It was the same song Victoria Miles had whistled after killing Uther. Inside of the box was a slip of paper with a message scrawled on it: *For some, death comes twice.* Panic raced through her body. Something felt wrong. Clarissa turned to run out of the stone door, but it was sliding shut.

"No!" She screamed and tried to pry the door back open. She wasn't strong enough.

Overhead, a panel began to slide open slowly. Sunlight filtered into the room where the ceiling had slid back. For the first time, Clarissa noticed piles of ash on the floor. She wasn't the first that this had happened to. She scanned the room for anything she could use as a shield from the sun. Nothing. There was nowhere for her to hide.

Her fists beat against the wall. There was no way anyone could hear her down here. She sank to her knees. How was she supposed to get out of here? Why would Uther have a map that led to death embroidered into the canopy of his bed? It was too much. The weight of her failure wracked her body. The hope inside of her escaped in a sob leaving behind only despair.

"How pathetic." A voice scoffed down at her. Clarissa looked up to see a dark-haired woman wearing leather peering down at her. She had only seen the woman's face once, but her features were seared into Clarissa's memory: Victoria Miles. The woman leapt agilely down to the floor of the room where Clarissa was. She made sure to stay in the wedge of sunlight slowly making its way across the space. "Do you like my music box? It was one of the last gifts my father ever gave me."

"Why are you doing this?!" Clarissa's face was red with desperation and rage.

"This room used to hold the cure for vampirism. It was woven into rumors and lore. The tree of life. Vampires weren't the only ones who knew about it. When your family has been in the slaying business long enough, they hear things." Victoria cleaned underneath her fingernails with the tip of a wooden stake. It was sharpened to a splinter on the end. She pulled a leather strap from around her neck. A small vial with green sap was on the end of it. A cruel smile distorted her face. "My great, great, grandfather found this place and took the cure. My family has been using it as a trap ever since."

"Why? If there is a cure, why wouldn't you want vampires to have it? If you're so against them, why wouldn't you want them to be human again?" Disbelief weighed down Clarissa's heart.

"Do you honestly think your kind deserves to be granted humanity? After all of the pain and anguish you reap on the world, do you think you deserve absolution for your actions? I believe in capital punishment for murderers, and deep down that is all you are."

"You're wrong." Clarissa stood shakily. She backed away from the sunlight that was encroaching slowly towards her. "Do you think I chose this?! I had to give up my life, my family, my job. I wasn't given a choice! Everything has been taken from me because some man liked the way my hair looked. But do you know what? You are worse than any vampire. You have the power to cure me, and instead you are condemning me to a life I never wanted. You are heartless."

Victoria tilted her head. "You know, I was going to make this quicker for you, but now I'm thinking I should just let you sizzle in the sun."

Clarissa backed up until she was pressed against the part of the wall furthest away from the light. The more sunlight came in, the harder it was for her to see. A grating noise made both women turn to look at the door leading to the tunnel Clarissa had entered from. The door was opening. A figure holding a flashlight stood in the shadows on the other side. Clarissa tried to peer past the beam of light, but her eyes couldn't look very long. The flashlight fell to the floor. Clarissa's vision was speckled with dots from looking at the light. She squinted and blinked repeatedly, trying to see what was happening.

"Run!" Clarissa recognized Cyrus's voice as he yelled to her.

The sunlight was touching her exit now. "I can't!"

She could hear scuffling and blows landing heavily on body parts. Victoria grunted as she punched Cyrus's face. "Don't think just because you're human I'm going to spare you. You gave up your humanity when you sided with them!"

Cyrus was on the ground with the wind knocked out of him. Clarissa squinted into the light. Something glinted in the sunlight. She didn't have time to think. The blade in Victoria's hand plunged towards Cyrus's chest. Clarissa threw herself into the light. Her body collided with the other woman's. Victoria was slammed against the wall. The slayer's impact was punctuated by a small shattering sound.

Sparks crackled along Clarissa's skin. Pure agony burned across her. Blisters bubbled up along her arms. She heard herself screaming, but it sounded far away. Tears of pain ran down her cheeks. The salt burned the cracks in her skin. Her lips split. Blood dribbled down her chin.

Suddenly, something was thrown over her. She was being dragged back into the safety of the dark tunnel. Clarissa's skin still felt like it was on fire, but the pain was numbing now. She looked at her shoulders to see the canopy fabric draped over her. Cyrus was looking behind them to the circular room. Turning gingerly, she followed his gaze.

Victoria was slumped on the ground. Blood gurgled up from her mouth in a crimson foam. The stake she had earlier was embedded in her chest. She must have impaled herself when Clarissa had slammed into her. Clarissa squinted into the brightness. Tiny shards of glass glinted on the floor. Green sap was smeared down the wall. The cure. Before her eyes, the sap began to dim in color until it was an inky black. The pain of burning in the sunlight was dwarfed by the devastation she felt now.

"Are you okay?" Cyrus scanned her face for an answer.

The blisters were starting to fade, but her body still ached. "It's gone."

"What? What's gone?"

"The cure." She felt her lips tremble, but she fought back more tears.

"At least you're still alive." His voice was harsher than he meant for it to be. He was still grieving.

"Is it really living though? The way that I am now?"

Cyrus pursed his lips together. "Stop. I just lost the man who raised me, and here you are pouting and thinking your life isn't worth living. Vampires can still do good things in this world. Me being here today is proof of that. You got dealt a crappy hand, but what you do now is what will define you. You can sulk and have an eternal pity party, or you can suck it up and make something of yourself."

She didn't want to listen to reason. "Do you want to know how I got here?" Clarissa pulled the canopy from around her shoulders and showed him the embroidery. "This map was stitched into the canopy of Uther's bed. He knew about the cure. He knew it existed, and he never acted on it. He never even told you about it."

"He must have had his reasons."

"How can you have so much blind faith in him?"

"Because that is what it means to love someone." Cyrus's voice broke as he spoke. "He was family to me. I trust his judgement." Cyrus turned to walk back down the hall.

She followed him slowly. Love. It seemed like such a foreign concept now. The thick, stone door slid shut one last time. Her body still ached from exposure. The walk back to the trap door in Uther's room seemed longer because of the silence between them. Knotted sheets dangled down from the opening. Cyrus climbed up first. Clarissa winced as she pulled herself up. Every movement hurt. He rolled his eyes and reached out a hand to help her. She took it and cried out as he pulled her out of the hole.

"Cyrus, I'm sorry." She knelt on the edge of the trap door. Regret fogged her mind.

"For what?" He wasn't letting her off the hook that easily.

"I'm dealing with a lot right now. It's not fair for me to take it out on you. You did save me back there after all."

"You saved me, too. She was going to kill me if you hadn't slammed into her."

Uther's words in her dream came back to her, "*Trust Cyrus. He's been with me long enough to know more about the world of vampires than any human should.*"

Clarissa couldn't look him in the eye. "I don't...I don't really have a support system anymore. Do you think you could help me transition? I mean, if it's not too much on you. I know you have your own stuff going on." She felt like a burden just asking for his help.

"How sweet." Emrick interrupted them before Cyrus could answer. He was leaning against the doorframe. "Uther's two little pets making alliances." His eyes landed on Clarissa's brittle and cracked skin. "Tried to get a tan, did we? Come with me."

The two of them followed him to the bar. He crushed up some pills and poured them into a shot glass of blood. "Drink this. It will help with the pain. You'll heal up by tomorrow if you take it easy. You need a steady supply of blood to heal properly."

Clarissa downed the drink. The pain killers absorbed into her bloodstream quickly. She sighed with relief. "You don't seem surprised by the trap door in Uther's bedroom."

"Why would I be? This is my home. I know everything about it."

"Did you know about the cure?" Cyrus butted into the conversation. No matter how much faith he had in Uther, he was still curious.

"Oh, that?" Emrick scoffed. "It's more of a curse than a cure. Can you imagine being given immortality and then having it stripped away from you? Plus, there are the side effects to consider."

"What side effects?" The pills were making her a little loopy, but she fought to focus on the conversation.

"You should always read the fine print on things like that. It will make you human again alright, but you would still be dead. Your body would begin to catch up to the decomposition it should have been at without vampirism. It's not a pretty picture. Actually, that is how Uther and I lost our sister. Uther had been trying to turn himself human again because he had Cyrus to look after. He thought the boy deserved as normal of a childhood as he could get. Uther always hated what he was and the way we had to survived. When he heard about the cure, Lyssa went with him to check it out. They were caught in a trap set up by Heath Miles, Victoria's father. They managed to get the cure away from him after they killed him. Lyssa tried it first because she wanted to make sure it worked. Older sisters are protective like that." A wry smile lingered on his lips for a moment before fading away. "Uther had to watch her decay before his eyes. He blamed himself for it, and Victoria grew up with a grudge against us. Her family pastime of killing vampires was exaggerated by her pent-up rage. There is no cure for what we are except death."

"That's why he never told me about it." Cyrus ran his hands through his dark hair.

"Yes, well, he always did try to protect you." Taking another sip of blood, Emrick wiped off his mouth. He raised his glass towards Clarissa. "You're welcome to stay here as long as you like. Cyrus on the other hand..."

"If he goes, I go." She held her chin up in the air.

"What is it about you that makes them want to pair up with you?" Emrick shook his head at Cyrus in disbelief. He sighed heavily. "Very well, but only because you are the last of my brother's line."

Clarissa walked slowly back towards Uther's old room. Cyrus's voice caught her off guard. "Yes."

"Yes?"

"Yes, I'll help you." His eyes traced her face.

The two of them shared a solemn smile before separating. Clarissa laid down gingerly in the bed. She stared at the naked ceiling while waiting for the pain killers to sweep her off to sleep. The ragged edges remaining from the canopy she had ripped down hung in frazzled ribbons. For the first time since she had become a vampire, she didn't feel alone. Her future wasn't just a gaping blackhole anymore. Now, there was a pinprick of light at the end of the tunnel. Uther may not have been able to completely make reparations for what he did, but he at least paved the way for her to have a fighting chance in her new life. After all, whether she wanted to view it as a curse or a blessing, now she had eternity to figure it out.

BLOODSHOT EYES

Bill Billingsley

Steam swirled up from the coffee cup in front of Ava. Her eyes were bloodshot from long nights at the police station. Dark circles dipped onto her cheeks. It had been a crazy couple of weeks. She laughed under her breath and shook her head.

"You ok there, Brooks?" Charlie poked his head out of his office.

"Yeah, yeah. I'm fine, Chief." Ava picked up her coffee cup and leaned back in her chair, "It's just still kind of surreal right now."

Charlie locked up his office door behind him, "We got him, kid. Go home and get some sleep, ok?"

"Yes, sir." Exhaustion spread over Ava's face as she sipped from her cup. Her coffee had made a ring around part of the morning paper's headline: *Green River Killer Captured.*

The Maple Valley Police Department had been working closely with the King County Sherriff's Office the past few years, but the murders had been going on for the past two decades. Young women murdered, their corpses violated. Some of the bodies still weren't identified yet. Most of them had been prostitutes. Ava's shoulders shuddered with a sigh of relief. The killer had been on the loose for most of her life. Even knowing he was behind bars, she still didn't feel safe. A lifetime spent looking over her shoulder, peering into dark alleyways, always making sure to park under a light. Those habits were drilled into her now. The fear of the unknown didn't vanish with a conviction. It lingered in the peripheral of her vision, waiting.

Patting her face to keep the delirium of sleep at bay, Ava grabbed her jacket and headed for the door. She paused in the doorway. The precinct was empty. Staplers were cockeyed on the corners of desks. Paperwork cluttered up baskets. The overhead lights buzzed softly. Ava leaned her forehead against the door frame and flipped off the light switch. She walked outside and locked the building behind her. The temperature was in the forties. Ava's breath clouded around her. The sudden cold helped to wake her up a bit. Her fingers fumbled in her pocket to find her car keys.

The key hole on the beat-up red Buick had a thin layer of frost over it. Ava shoved the key into the door and pried it open. It took a few moments for the frosted windshield to thaw. Her hands ached from the cold. She buried them between her legs for extra warmth until the car had enough visibility to drive. Streetlights pierced the night and burst in halos on the glass. She couldn't see any stars.

Ava's duplex was dark as she pulled into the driveway. Her neighbors were out of town for an early Christmas vacation. She scraped her boots on the door mat and flicked on the stained glass lamp to the right of the door.

"Hey, Simon," the orange tabby weaved in and out of her legs leaving cat fur on her uniform. "Sorry I was out again so late."

Ava poured some cat food in his bowl. She put her badge and gun on the counter next to a bowl of badly bruised bananas. A soft smile lingered on her lips as her eyes lit upon an old picture of her mother. It was a bittersweet moment. The wrinkles on her mom's face showed a lifetime of hard decisions. Ava had never met her dad. As far as she knew he could have been any of the Johns her mom had to turn to put food on the table. She wasn't proud of it, but she did what she had to in order to make sure she and Ava were taken care of. That's why the Green River Killer had been such an important case. In every victim's face, Ava saw her mother. Any one of those girls could have been a struggling single mom just trying to get by.

Downing a beer from the fridge, Ava stumbled towards her bedroom. "Come on, Simon. Let's hit the hay."

The two-day weekend went by way too fast. Monday morning, Ava geared up and headed back to the station. Simon sat in the living room window, tail flicking back and forth as she backed out of the driveway. The road to the station was clear of traffic. The city seemed more at ease after Ridgway was behind bars. Ava's heart skipped a beat as she pulled into her parking space. The medical examiner's car was parked out front.

The bell dinged signaling her entrance, "Hey, Reyes, why is Mike here?" She peered across the office to where the medical examiner was spreading out some pictures on the back table.

"You didn't hear yet?" Andre Reyes pushed out of his chair so he could talk lower, "Another body came up over the weekend."

"Do they think it was another GRK victim?"

Reyes shrugged, "That's the thing. Fits the pattern, but get this, M.E. places time of death two days after Ridgway was arrested."

Ava's face contorted in panic concern, "Do you think he wasn't the real killer?"

"He confessed." Reyes shook his head, "Most likely copycat killer or maybe an accomplice."

Walking briskly, Ava approached the table at the back of the room where the Chief and a few other officers were looking over crime scene pictures with Mike. She picked up one of the pictures. A young woman, no older than twenty-five was tinged blue. Her eyes were wide open. A fly had landed on her pupil when the camera had taken the image. She was naked like the rest of the victims. The picture churned Ava's stomach, "Why weren't we called when it happened?"

"Sent it to the King County Sheriffs first to have the Green River Task Force take a look at it. Seemed like something they would want to know about." Mike shook his grey head. "You know, I was hoping we were done with this now."

Charlie patted him on the back, "Go get you some coffee. I'll fill Officer Brooks in."

Ava watched Mike walk away before she spoke, "Chief, what if we got the wrong guy?"

"He confessed, Brooks. Working on a plea bargain."

"But this fits the pattern."

Charlie massaged the worry lines on his forehead, "Except for one thing. Look at her closer. What do you see?"

Studying the pictures closer, Ava wracked her brain. "She's clean."

"Yup. The last few we found were buried. Ridgway said he started burying them so he wouldn't be tempted to have sex with the bodies later. This one wasn't buried."

"Any DNA on her?"

"There was some vaginal tearing, but the culprit wore a condom, so no semen." Charlie leaned his head to the side as a voice rang out over the radio on his shoulder.

"Charlie, I think you're going to want to see this." Static crackled over the radio.

"What is it?" The Chief held down the button on the side as he replied.

"We've got three more."

Ava's heart dropped into her stomach. The drive out to the river bank made her want to throw up. Four more girls had died since Ridgway had been off the streets. Boots squelched through the mud as officers combed the fallen branches at the river's edge for any clues or evidence. Three girls were laying side by side near a pile of rocks. One of them still had pink in her cheeks. This was a fresh dump.

"Son of a—" Ava kicked a half-rotted tree stump.

"Brooks, go take five!" The Chief yelled out admonishingly and pointed to where the cruisers were parked.

Waving her arms in frustration, she stomped back to her car and paced along the side. This couldn't keep happening! So many girls had died already, and they were so close to wrapping everything up. Now there was another killer on the loose. She couldn't just sit here and watch this keep happening in her town anymore. It had eaten away at her for the last two years. Charlie had kept telling her the Task Force had the lead on this one. This was their territory. But now? The Green River Killer was behind bars now. This was a new killer. Up for grabs.

"Brooks, you doing ok?" Reyes sat on the hood of her police car.

"I can't keep doing this, Andre."

"Well, what do you have in mind?" He ran his hand through his dark brown hair and looked at her while she moved frantically back and forth.

Ava pursed her lips, "I'm sick of us playing tag along. What if we've been going about this the wrong way? Going from body to body waiting on the next victim...We need to get in front of this. We need to get someone on the inside."

"How?" There was a slight scoff to his voice.

"What if someone went undercover?"

"Who would be dumb enough—" Andre paused, "No. No way. You can't put yourself at risk like that."

"We put ourselves at risk every day!"

"Not like that. That would be walking into a lion's den."

"I can't sit on the sidelines anymore." Ava bit her bottom lip and looked back towards the river bank, "Someone has to help them."

Charlie was taking long strides in their direction, "You calmed down any?"

"Put me under cover." Ava's voice was brash and brazen. Her eyes shone out fiercely. Rocks rolled under her feet as she took a more authoritative stance. Feet apart, shoulders back.

Wrinkles and bristly eyebrows matted across the Chief's brow, "Ava, I know these cases are important to you." His voice was gentle and compassionate, "But right now you're too emotionally involved. I can't put you out in the field like this." He shook his head apologetically, "I can't have that on my conscience."

Charlie turned and walked back towards the river bank. Hot tears brimmed in Ava's eyes. She could do this! She *needed* to do this. She felt sick in her stomach that she had put herself out on a limb and been turned down. It was like the Chief was telling her she wasn't good enough. Her teeth ground into one another as she watched him walk away. She was strategically avoiding Andre's gaze. If she made eye contact the dam inside her would burst, and her tears would overwhelm her.

They stood there in silence for a moment. The sound of rushing water mingled with the braying barks of the K-9 unit. A frigid breeze cut across their cheeks. Andre shifted his weight on the hood of the car, "You know he cares about you, right?"

"Sometimes I wish he didn't." Ava climbed in her police car and threw it in reverse. Andre leapt off of the hood and staggered a few steps away as she spun out of the gravel clearing driving back towards town.

Charlie had been like a dad to her even before her mom had passed away. She had lost count of how many times he had tried to get her mom to get her life together. She never brought the men home with her, so at least there was that, but between the bruises and the track marks Adeline Brooks had been fighting a losing battle. Charlie was the one who had come to the house the morning her mother died to break the news. Heroin overdose. Since then, the officers had been Ava's second family. They made sure she was taken care of, and not long after her mom's passing, Ava applied to the police academy. Fresh out of high school and determined not to make her mother's mistakes, she sailed through the obstacle courses and classes. Years later she still felt like she had to prove she was worthy to be on the force. The chip on her shoulder from Adeline's death still weighed heavily on her. If she had been a stronger daughter, maybe she could have helped her mom stay clean. If she had gotten an after-school job, maybe her mom wouldn't have had to sell herself to pay the rent. Ava blamed herself for the depression that overtook Adeline and pushed her towards the dependency. A single mom with no support system. The pressure and isolation had eventually led to the overdose.

Stopped at a red light in town, Ava saw a young woman dressed in skimpy attire duck around the corner of a building. She was getting off the street at the sight of the cruiser. Trying to avoid a confrontation.

She had to be freezing in this weather. Smoke trailed up from a cigarette butt the girl had dropped on the sidewalk. When the light turned green, Ava passed the gap between buildings the girl had disappeared into. There were a few other girls in there with her. All of them were in short skirts and low-cut tops, shivering in the alley. Ava's fingers tightened on the steering wheel. She hadn't been able to save her mother, but she could still save these girls.

Simon purred happily around her feet as she walked into the living room. Ava punched in Charlie's number as she walked to her bedroom and flung open her closet. She flipped through the hangers holding her uniforms until she was at the far end. "Hey, Charlie, it's Brooks. I was thinking about what you said earlier, and I think it might be good for me to take a few weeks off and clear my head." Her fingers closed on a hanger holding a leopard print miniskirt. "Mmmhmm, ok. Thanks, Chief." The line went dead. Ava pulled out the miniskirt and a button-up blouse.

The next day, Ava put on extra make-up and pulled the skirt into place. She was going undercover even if she had to do it on her own. She had dropped her cruiser off at the station yesterday. Today she opened the garage and backed her mom's old, blue Toyota out. It was ancient, but less recognizable than her own red car. Dust coated the dash board, and the engine churned a few times before it started up. Adeline's favorite radio station boomed to life. Ava turned the radio down and headed for a parking lot behind the old pool joint. Goosebumps scaled her skin as she stepped out into the cold and sauntered over to the alley near the side door that led into the pool hall. A girl with ratted blonde hair and sunken eyes was leaning against the brick wall.

"Hey!" The girl pushed off from the wall and made a beeline for Ava, "This is my spot. You go get your own!" The girl pulled a knife out of her bag and flicked it open.

Ava staggered backwards, "Whoa, hey. I'm just...I'm just trying to score some H, ok?" Ava made her voice raspy and slowed her normal speaking rate. "I just need some H or some cash so I can pay a guy." She nodded her head down like she had seen her mother do countless times.

The girl paused and looked Ava up and down before putting her knife away, "You trying to get heroine?"

"Yeah, yeah, that's what I said, you know?" Ava's heart was racing already.

"Alright, ok. I'll make you a deal." The girl licked her lips. "You can stay, and any money we make will go to me. Any guy that's got H, you can have it. And," the girl scratched her arm, "if we don't get any heroine, I'll give you enough for your next hit, alright?"

It was a shit deal, but a junkie would do anything for the next fix, "Alright." Ava nodded her head and smiled goofily. "I'm Ava, by the way."

"Steph." The blonde walked back over to the wall and leaned against it again.

"How many guys you get a day here?" Ava fidgeted with her hair.

"Depends. Some days one or two. Some five or six. Business usually picks up around the holidays. Guys start feeling lonely and need a little extra comfort."

Cars drove by on the street. Steph took a few drags off of a cigarette and crossed her arms. Ava watched her from the corner of her eye, "You got family?"

"Nah. Mom's in jail for killing my dad. Only child. You?"

"Just my cat."

"Ya know, maybe it's better that way. Animals are the best kind of people." Steph smiled with the cigarette between her lips. "What's its name?"

"Simon."

"Had a turtle once. Dad found it on the side of the road. That was the only pet I ever had growing up. Named him Soup."

"You named your turtle Soup?" Ava laughed.

Steph shrugged her shoulders, "Dark sense of humor."

A black car pulled up behind the pool hall and rolled down its window. Steph walked over to the window and leaned down. Ava saw her take a wad of cash and stuff it in her bag before opening the door. She looked over her shoulder and mouthed, 'back in ten.' Ava's stomach churned. She didn't want to let Steph go with this guy knowing there was a killer on the loose, but if she said anything she would blow her cover. Ava held her breath as the car pulled out of the parking lot. She memorized the license plate as he drove out of sight.

It was unnerving that girls would just climb into a stranger's car and perform sexual acts with them. This is what her mom had done. It made her sick to think about it. Maybe Charlie was right. Maybe she was too emotionally involved in this. Shaking her head, Ava took a deep breath to steady her nerves. She needed to fight down that urge to flee and hold on to her anger.

Ten minutes seemed like an hour by the time Steph got back to the alley way. She pulled some lip balm out of her bag and rubbed it on her lips. She held out her hand and offered it to Ava, "Want some?"

"Uh, no thanks," Ava shook her head disinterestedly. Guiltily, she pushed back the thought that she might get herpes if she shared ChapStick with this girl.

"Anybody come by while I was gone?"

"Nope."

Steph tugged her skirt back down a little more, "Good."

The sun was starting to go down. After-work traffic flooded the busy street on one side of the alley. Inside the pool hall they could hear balls bouncing off of tables, and rock music hummed through the walls. Ava's arms and legs were numb. She and Steph had naturally huddled closer to one another to try and conserve body heat. Headlights reflected off of the side of a dumpster beside them. The driver flashed the lights. Steph's teeth chattered as she walked over to the car. Ava could tell she and the driver were discussing something. Steph didn't seem too happy about whatever it was.

After a minute, Steph stood up and walked back over to Ava. "This guy wants to do doubles." She looked as though she had taken a drink of spoiled milk, "Look, I haven't ever done a double before, but he's willing to pay extra for us both."

Ava's intuition was curdling at the sight of this car. She couldn't see inside, but something felt off. She nodded her head and bit her lip. Steph couldn't go off alone with this guy, "Ok, yeah."

"Yeah?" Steph looked surprised and a little relieved.

"Yeah," Ava repeated herself with more conviction.

The two girls walked to the car together. Ava fought her instinct to run. Steph climbed in the front seat as Ava slid in the back. The guy in the driver's seat was wearing wire rimmed glasses. He had thick blonde hair combed over to one side. His face was more handsome than Ava had been expecting. She always thought of Johns as slightly overweight, balding, middle aged men. This guy was probably in his thirties. The interior of the car smelled of leather with a faint hint of fast food. His eyes locked on Ava through the rearview mirror. He adjusted his glasses. Trying to hide her discomfort, Ava massaged warmth back into her arms. The car's heater was the only part about this that was even remotely comforting. Charlie would kill her if he knew she was doing this.

"Where are we going?" Steph tugged her seatbelt into a more comfortable position.

"Not far," the driver's voice was a soft tenner. The mildness of his tone caught Ava off guard.

They drove until they reached an abandoned lumber mill. He put the car in park, and Steph unbuckled her seatbelt. She reached over to his lap and started to undo his pants, but he grabbed her wrist. Ava's heart beat quicker as she watched from the backseat. She didn't want to see this, much less participate. What had she gotten herself into?

"Not here," he placed Steph's hand back in her own lap and climbed out of the car.

"Well, where do you want to do this? It's freezing out there!" The sun had almost disappeared as Steph tried to keep the rendezvous contained in the car.

"I want to go inside." He jerked his head towards the door of the lumber mill, "I'm paying you well enough. Get your assess inside."

"You've got to be kidding me." Steph rolled her eyes and shoved her door open with an exasperated sigh.

Ava opened her door warily. The dirt parking lot was packed solid. The temperature was dropping even more. The guy motioned for her and Steph to go through the rusted metal door. The hairs on the back of Ava's neck were standing up. This was bad. There was little light in the building. Streams of fading sunlight crept through cracks in the walls. It smelled like sawdust and mold. Steph shuddered beside her. As Ava's eyes adjusted to the dim interior, she heard a small click behind her. The sound froze her in place.

"Get on your knees." The guy pressed the barrel of a gun to Ava's back.

"Oh shit!" Steph whispered weakly, half turning her head to see what was happening. Her voice broke, "Please, please don't. We'll do whatever you want for free, ok?"

"Shut up and get on your knees!" He turned the gun on Steph who choked back a sob.

Ava slowly sank to her knees. Cold cement bit into her kneecaps and shins. The man circled around them. Ava's eyes darted around the room trying to find anything she might be able to use as a weapon. A few shoddy pieces of two by four were scattered a few feet away. A wooden pallet was propped against the side of the building. Nothing in arm's reach. She closed her eyes and tried to calm herself down enough to think. The sound of a zipper unzipping made her open her eyes. The man was fondling himself inside of his pants. Ava cringed and looked away. She had to think of something to get them out of here.

"Come here," he motioned for Steph to move closer.

Sobbing softly, Steph scooted closer to him. Ava heard the man sigh followed by slight sucking noises. She forced herself to glance up. The man had one hand on the back of Steph's head, and the other with the gun was resting on the top of his own head. His eyes were closed. Steph gagged and tried to pull away from him, but he kept her where she was. Ava was able to catch Steph's eye. Tears were streaming down her face. She looked terrified. With one more glance to make sure his eyes were still closed, Ava made a silent chomping gesture with her teeth. Steph's fear was causing her to shake. Ava could see her struggling to muster the will power before she opened her mouth wider and clamped her jaw down. A shot rang out as the man squeezed the trigger automatically, his body recoiling in pain. He screamed in utter agony, and blood spurted from where Steph's teeth had ripped through him.

Before he could recover, Ava charged at his knees and knocked him onto his back. The gun skittered across the floor. He was having trouble breathing, and his arms fought more to curl towards his wound than they did to get Ava off of him. She managed to flip him over and pull his arms behind his back. Her foot pressed into the center of his back. The pain became too much, and his body went limp. Blood slowly spread across the floor near his waist. Steph was spitting profusely trying to get the taste out of her mouth. She was shaking from adrenaline and from the cold.

"Find his phone!" Ava yelled at Steph to bring her back to the moment.

"I-I don't know where it is!" The girl fumbled through his pockets, "We need to leave. We gotta get out of here!" Her numb fingers finally wrestled the phone out of his left pocket.

"Call the police," Ava's own breathing was shuddering now.

"Are you crazy?! They'll send us to jail! We're a prostitute and a junkie. They'll never believe us!"

"I'm a cop! Call them."

"What? Holy shit. Holy shit!" Steph punched in the number and ran her fingers through her hair, pacing nervously. "Yes, hello? There was—I'm—" She pulled the phone away from her face and looked at Ava in panic, "I don't know what to say!"

Ava jerked the phone from her hand, "This is Officer Ava Brooks. I need Maple Valley P.D. at the old lumber mill. Suspect was injured during apprehension. Send an ambulance!" She tossed the phone to the ground. "Steph, I need you to remain calm, ok? Can you do that for me?"

"You're a freaking cop! Listen, Ava, please don't send me to jail, please! I didn't mean to hurt him that bad, I was just so scared."

"Calm down! He had a gun on us. It was self-defense." Ava needed to get her calm. She was starting to hyperventilate, "Just breathe, ok?"

"Ok," Steph took deep, ragged breaths trying to regain her composure.

Within minutes, police sirens echoed in the distance followed by an ambulance. Charlie came through the door with his gun drawn, "Put your hands up!" He barked his order at Steph and glanced to Ava. Over Steph's renewed panic, he called out to Ava, "What happened? You were supposed to be on vacation!"

"I lied!" Ava yelled back as two EMT's came in to assess the man's wounds. Grabbing Charlie's handcuffs, she secured the man's wrists behind his back before she let go of him. "I had to do this, Chief. I couldn't sit back and let more women die because of sick people like this guy!" Out of the corner of her eye, she saw Reyes bag the suspect's gun for evidence.

"Well what the hell happened here?" Charlie's face was red with anger.

"I put myself undercover and ran into Steph," Ava gestured to the blonde girl the EMT's were leading outside with a blanket wrapped around her. "This John wanted us both to go with him, and when we got here he pulled a gun on us. Forced Steph into oral sex, and she bit him out of self-defense."

Charlie winced, "Jezuz, Brooks." He shook his head.

"Hey, Chief? You might want to come over here." Reyes called out.

Ava and Charlie walked to where Andre's voice had come from. He was standing behind a pile of rotted two-by-fours. A girl was laying behind the wood pile. She couldn't be more than seventeen. Reyes leaned down and pressed his fingers into her neck. There was a faint pulse beneath his fingertips.

"I need an EMT over here now!" Andre's voice boomed across the room.

A woman in scrubs ran over to them and started taking vitals. "She's still alive, but barely." Surprise echoed in her voice as she sprang into action.

"It has to be him!" Ava shot darts with her eyes towards the unconscious man being bandaged.

"We don't know that yet." Charlie shook his head at her again.

Ava stared at him incredulously, "Seriously! Look where we are! Look at this girl!"

"It's all circumstantial right now. We must have something to tie him to this and the other murders. We can't convict him just because he brought you to where an almost dead girl was."

"Check his car! Check through here! There has to be something." Ava's frustration was seizing her chest.

"Reyes, get her out of here. Take her home." Charlie waved her away dismissively. His actions were like a dagger in her heart.

Reyes pulled off his jacket and slung it over Ava's shoulders. It was still warm as she pulled her arms into it, "What do you think?" She climbed sullenly into the passenger seat of Andre's car.

"Well," he fired up the heater and pulled away from the old lumber mill, "I think even if he isn't the guy we've been looking for, you still helped to get a bad person off of the street. I think those two girls are only alive right now because of you. Try not to let Chief get to you, ok?"

Ava stewed in her anger and aggravation, "I just want so badly to make a difference here."

"To those girls you made a hell of a difference."

"I just don't want anyone else to die."

A half smile curved Andre's lips, "That's why most of us become policemen. To stop the bad guys. Save people. You're too hard on yourself." He glanced over at her.

"What do you think is going to happen now?"

"We'll just have to see what the evidence says. Who knows? Maybe you did help catch the second killer."

Andre dropped Ava off at home. Simon greeted her as usual. As the headlights backed out of her drive, Ava scooped up Simon and let herself cry into his fur. Her arms were still shaking. Her mom had put herself in those kinds of situations all the time to take care of her. She cried from exhaustion and emotional stress. She cried because even if this guy was the killer, she would still feel inadequate inside. Ava thought if she could save lives she would finally feel worthy of her badge, but right now all she felt was small and alone. Simon purred contentedly in her lap. Eventually, she cried herself to sleep still wearing Andre's jacket.

The next few days were stressful. She had been cut off from knowing what was going on in the investigation. Her statement had been videotaped and reviewed. She wasn't allowed to know the evidence surrounding the case since technically she had been working against orders. Andre was coming over after his shift today to pick up his jacket. Ava scrambled to gather up the half-empty beer bottles around her duplex before he came over.

A car pulled into the driveway followed by Andre's knock. Ava called through the door, "Come in!"

He stepped inside and wiped his feet on the mat. Simon flicked his tail sleepily on the back of the couch, "Hey."

"Any news?"

Andre scowled slightly, "Can't really tell you much, but the girl we found woke up today."

"How's she doing?"

"Alright, considering." He shrugged and sat down on the couch. Simon's tail curled casually around Andre's face. Reyes tried to shoo the tail away, but Simon was persistent.

"Any idea when they are going to charge him, or if they are going to charge him?"

Andre nodded, "D.A. is talking with him. They think we should know more in a few days."

"Ok." Ava frowned and picked up his jacket, "Sorry, it's got some cat hair on it."

"Eh, that's alright." Andre pushed himself up and took the jacket from her.

"Thanks for loaning it to me the other night, by the way."

"No problem." Andre waved goodbye and headed out the door. Ava followed and closed it behind him.

The next day she received a call from Charlie asking her to come down to the police station. Her stomach tossed and turned the whole way there. She hadn't really been able to eat too much since the night everything happened. Ava took a deep breath and trudged into the station. A few people stared at her as she walked in. Other avoided looking at her all together. She bit her lip and rapped her knuckles on the Chief's door.

"Yep, come in." He was shuffling through paperwork as she walked into his office. He glanced up at her, "Close the door behind you."

"What's going on, Chief?" Ava closed the door with a click behind her and sat across from Charlie.

"Well, Brooks, I wanted to be the first to tell you that the man you apprehended—Elan Parker—confessed to the murders of those four girls we found."

A sigh of relief exploded from Ava, "I *knew* it had to be him!"

"Hang on, I'm not done yet."

"Yes, sir. Sorry, sir." She tucked her hand into her lap and looked at the tops of her knees.

"Turns out that Parker attended the same church as Ridgway. Shared some of his same ideals. Once Ridgway was arrested, Parker took it on himself to," Charlie motioned with air quotes, "carry on the vision and rid the world of the unclean women." He mumbled under his breath, "Self-righteous prick."

"So what happens now?"

"Well, he's going to jail. D.A. is just battering around details of his sentence now. Trying to see if he can help find any other victims that Ridgway may not have revealed yet."

"Ok," Ava nodded determinedly. She felt as though she had made some progress towards proving herself.

"Parker isn't the only reason I wanted to talk to you today."

Ava's heart sank from the pain that crossed momentarily across the Chief's face. "What is it?" Apprehension filled her gut.

"You went directly against my orders in doing this, Ava. You put yourself and members of the public in danger because of your actions."

"I saved two girls' lives!" Ava pushed away from the desk and stood up.

"I know," he held his hands up defensively, "but that doesn't change the fact that you went against orders. I have to suspend you."

"Unbelievable! I helped you find a killer before he killed anyone else." She leaned down towards him. Her blood was boiling.

"Brooks, I'm going to have to ask you to watch your tone." Charlie stood up, towering above her.

Ava clenched her jaw and shook her head, "I can't believe this. How long is my suspension?"

"Two months."

"Two months! Are you kidding me?"

"During that time, I set up a place for you to volunteer at the Vine Maple Place. I think it might help you get in touch with your core beliefs a little better. You also have to see a psychologist to deal with any residual trauma from that night in the lumber mill, and honestly maybe some issues you're having still from the loss of your mother."

Vine Maple Place was an organization that helped families find their feet after hardships. It also helped kids that were on the path to living on the street. Kids that might one day end up like Steph if not for some extra help. Ava nodded and left his office in silence.

Maybe Charlie was right. Maybe this was what she needed right now. Volunteering there would give her a sense of accomplishment and the knowledge that she was making a difference in the lives of those families. It was more of an immediate spiritual reward than trailing a criminal from body to body and just hoping to stop them before someone else was killed. She knew she was meant to make a difference in the world. She had come too far to fall under the shadow of the heartache that men like Ridgway and Parker cast. She was determined to fight against the current.

THE CREEPING

66

JESSICA BLACK

Strings of seashells clinked daintily in the breeze of the hut. Dried palm leaves stretched their fingers over the edge of the roof. The setting sun cast flitting red shadows along the curve of the lagoon. Waves lapped ravenously at the sand. Kristen swallowed hard. This was the place.

"Are you sure about this?" Ty stood beside her. His toes slipped between the sand dunes as he looked down at her.

Kristen nodded and edged closer to the door of the hut. She raised her hand to knock on the door, but before she touched it, the door swung open. A woman with dark plaited hair stood in the doorway, "Come in." Her teeth gleamed like a white crescent moon against her lips.

Crossing the threshold, Kristen fished out a week-old cutting from the local paper from her back pocket, "We're here about—"

"I know why you're here." The woman cut her off and whisked the slip of paper out of the girl's fingers. She studied it with narrowed eyes. Her fingertips curled around the edges.

The paper showed a black and white photo from the front page of the newspaper. Framed in the center was Cali's body, washed up on the gritty shore of Salacia Lagoon. A circlet of seaweed had washed up near her hand. The picture didn't show the way the sunlight used to kiss her skin, or the way that her wet hair used to form a heart around her face when she burst through the surface for air. No, in this picture she wasn't Cali anymore. She was just another empty shell that had washed upon the shore.

"I will need something that had a connection to the girl."

"We don't really have—oh! Wait." Kristen touched the faded bracelet on her wrist, "She made this for me." Her eyes searched the woman's.

Long fingers deftly loosened the bracelet from the girl's wrist, "It will do." The woman gazed intently at the picture and rubbed the fabric of the bracelet between her fingers. Breathing deeply in and out, she slowly walked out of the hut. Her bare feet left imprints behind her. Her eyes were closed as she walked.

"Are we supposed to follow her?" Ty hissed out of the corner of his mouth so only Kristen could hear him.

"I don't know. I guess so."

"This was your idea!"

"It's not like I've done this before either!" Kristen exclaimed in an agitated whisper. The woman was already halfway down the beach. The two teenagers hurriedly followed after her.

When the woman got to the edge of the water by a log, she paused. "This is where her life ended." Sadness hollowed her words.

"We already knew that. You could tell that by the picture." Ty shook his head in aggravation and grabbed Kristen's arm, "Come on, let's go. This was a waste of time."

Kristen shook him off, "No." She glared at him reproachfully before turning back to the woman before them, "I'm sorry. He doesn't really believe in this kind of thing." She smiled sheepishly, still holding out hope that this woman could help them find out what had really happened.

"Skepticism is healthy in a world of smoke and mirrors. I do not fault you for that, Ty."

At her words, Ty looked up alarmed, "How did you know my name?"

"It is one of my gifts. I'm sure my own name has been whispered more than once among the children of the town."

Kristen offered shyly, "They call you Hedda the voodoo woman in town."

"Ha!" A dry laugh escaped Hedda's lips. "They tie such ugly words to what they don't understand. In your parents' generation, it was Hedda Hoodoo. I do no more voodoo than you do. No, what I do is something much more connected."

"What do you do, then?" Kristen's voice was barely audible above the waves.

Hedda tilted her head to the side as if to jostle the right word into her mouth, "I prefer to call it parapsychology."

"What's that?" Ty crossed his arms over his chest.

"Well, if psychology is the study of the human mind, then parapsychology is a step beyond that. Imagine that you are a spider, and every choice you make leaves behind a thin thread. If someone could see that thread, they could follow your choices and be able to see how you affect the world. There are different ways to follow the threads and to interpret them. Some people can even see tentative threads of possible choices that have yet to be made. Not everyone can see them, but for those who can, the world becomes a tapestry of tiny threads all woven together into something much bigger than ourselves."

"That sounds like a load of bull."

"Ty!" Kristen smacked him with the back of her hand.

Hedda simply smiled, "Would you like me to show you?" She held out the hand that still had Kristen's friendship bracelet in it.

Ty looked at her uncertainly, he wanted to say no, but it was almost like his hand was moving of its own accord. As his hand touched hers, memories washed over him. The world around him faded as his mind pulled up one of his favorite memories of Cali.

"Come on, Ty!" Cali's blonde hair streamed behind her. It was barely summer, but the sun had already bleached highlights into her long, straight hair. The sun was setting on the water. Her laugh trailed behind her, "I'm going to win!"

He had let her beat him to the waves. The sand kicked up by her heels peppered his thighs. Ty watched as she pulled off her shirt like she always did at this point. Even though he knew what to expect, his heart still skipped a beat. Underneath was her pink bikini top. Cali always wore her swimsuit under her clothes in the summer, just in case. She screamed in happiness as the cold water climbed up her body. He plunged in after her. The cold seized his lungs. Cali ducked under the water to wet her hair and popped back up as he waded closer to her. The water weighed down her hair and outlined her face in a heart.

"Hold still." He brushed a strand of hair away from her eyes. She beamed up at him. Water pearled on her eyelashes. As she looked up at him, he felt himself drawn in. Her face came closer to his—

"No!" Ty verbally tried to shake himself out of the memory as his body recoiled. He couldn't go through that again right now. His heart couldn't take it. He pulled his hand away from Hedda's.

"Good memories do not die with the people who created them, Ty. She wouldn't want you to lock them away."

"Don't talk like you knew her!" His fingernails dug into his palms. The memory had seemed so real. *She* had seemed so real.

"So, can you help us?" Kristen looked back and forth between her friend and Hedda. She wasn't sure what had just happened, but Ty's face was pale.

"I can try." Hedda sat down in the sand and held out her hands to them. "We will need to make a circle."

Kristen sat on one side of Hedda and placed her hand on top of the woman's. She looked up at Ty pleadingly, "Please, Ty?"

"Fine." Letting out a sigh of disapproval, Ty sank to the sand completing the circle between Kristen and Hedda.

Once their hands were joined, Hedda closed her eyes, "I need you to both clear your minds and picture Cali. Remember the way she smelled. The way her voice sounded. The more vivid you picture her, the easier it will be for me to contact her."

For a moment, nothing happened. Suddenly, a wave of energy washed over them. Warmth pulsed through the three of them. The hairs on their arms began to stand on end. Hedda held their hands tighter.

A picture formed in their minds. Cali was running. It was different this time. She was afraid. Ty's heart constricted. He tried to reach out to her, but Hedda held on tighter to his hand. There was no sound. It was like suddenly being in a soundproof room. Cali turned and stumbled backwards towards the water. Her hands flew in front of her face. They could see her scream, but it was silent. A blurred figure entered the vision for a split second. They saw Cali start to fall.

Kristen pulled away, breaking the circle. She was gasping for breath. Her lips trembled, "What was that?"

Hedda's shoulders slumped in exhaustion, "That was some of Cali's final moments."

"Are you ok?" Ty placed his hand on Kristen's shoulder.

"Yeah," she nodded, but her heart was still pounding furiously under her ribs. "Hedda?" She looked at the woman in concern. Kristen carefully took the picture and the bracelet back.

"I need to rest. It takes a lot of energy to see something like that and share it with you as well." She wobbled to her feet. Kristen ducked under one of her arms and motioned for Ty to do the same. With Hedda supported between them, they trudged back to her hut.

"What do you need us to do?" Propping the door open, Kristen guided her into the hut.

"I just need to rest. Come back tomorrow." Hedda waved them weakly away as she grabbed a bottle and sipped from it. She laid down on the rickety wooden bed in the corner and draped a cool cloth over her eyes.

Ty pulled Kristen back outside. "We shouldn't even be here."

"She is the only one who is even trying to help us! We have to try, Ty."

"We tried. We still don't know what really happened to Cali. If anything, what happened tonight only brought up more questions."

"Well, I'm not ready to give up! She wouldn't have given up on us." Kristen held up the picture for him to see again. He grabbed the slip of paper from her fingers. Ty crumpled up the image and tossed it angrily towards the side of Hedda's hut. "Hey!" Kristen scampered after the balled-up piece of paper. Small sand dunes nipped at her flipflops. "Why did you do that?" Pain and anguish contorted her face. She was still in denial.

"What's the point? She's gone." Ty's dirty blonde bangs fell over his eyes like a veil.

Trying desperately to smooth out the wrinkles, Kristen clutched the image to her chest, "It just...it matters."

"Sometimes, people just die. Accidents happen."

"No, not to Cali. Not like that. She was the strongest swimmer of all of us, and she never would have gone out at night like that. Not alone." Kristen's voice trembled. "How can you say that?"

Ty sighed and pulled Kristen into a hug. Her shoulders heaved against his chest. "I'm sorry, Kris. I'm just angry."

"Who do you think it was that was chasing her?" Her voice was muffled against his shirt. Her hot breath warmed him.

"I don't know."

"Will you come back with me, tomorrow?"

The small note of hope on the end of her question made his heart ache, "Sure, Kris. I'll come back with you tomorrow." He felt defeated. After losing Cali, he couldn't take this away from her, too. Hedda was their last hope. The police had written off the death as a swimming accident, but both he and Kristen knew better. The whole ordeal had just felt off to them.

The night had passed with little sleep to be had. Every time he closed his eyes, he could see Cali's face. It morphed from her laughing and looking up at him to screaming from someone chasing her. A light tapping sound pinged the glass on his window early the next morning. He looked down into the yard to see Kristen waiting for him. Throwing on some shorts and a gently used shirt, he tiptoed down the stairs and out the back door.

"Did your mom see?" Kristen bit her bottom lip.

Ty shook his head and rubbed his eyes, "No, she's not up yet."

"I couldn't sleep."

"Me either."

They walked in silence down the stone path towards the beach. Birds twittered in nearby bushes. The sky was grey, and a light breeze stirred the sand across their path. Hedda's hut was tucked away further down the beach. A palm tree loomed up beside it. The door was propped open, and they could smell something floral coming from inside.

"Come in, children." Hedda's voice called out to them as the house came into view. The shells strung along the roof clicked together.

"How are you feeling?" Kristen was the first to walk inside again. Ty strayed behind her.

"As well as can be expected. Today may be harder on you than it is on me."

"What do you mean?" Ty eyed the mugs she was pouring something into.

"Today we are going to try to approach Cali through dream telepathy." She handed each of them a cup. "This is chamomile tea with some valerian root added. It will help soothe your mind and body into a more restful state. It's not a terrible potion, Ty, so get that look off of your face. It is only some tea with a natural root added."

"How is this supposed to help us find out what happened to Cali?" Kristen sniffed her cup.

Hedda smiled to herself, "Most people possess some ability to tap into knowledge that they don't quite understand. It can be a gut feeling that tells you which answer is correct on a test, or it can be simply knowing who is on the other end of the phone before you even answer it. Most people write it off as coincidence or a lucky guess. Others seek to hone those skills. When you are awake, your mind is overloaded with signals from the world around you: smell, sound, taste, sight. When you are asleep, your subconscious is able to work through those signals and experiences in the forms of dreams. Almost all dreams have some sort of parceled up information that you are trying to deal with, even if you don't know what it is. You will both drink the tea and try to picture Cali as clearly in your mind as you can. I will try to guide you through the process, and if it seems like your dreams are getting too dangerous, I will be here to wake you up."

"Are you sure this is safe?" Kristen clutched the cup in her hands. Her worried eyes reflected in the surface of the drink.

"Nothing worth knowing or having is ever truly easy or safe."

"It's for Cali." Ty tipped back is cup and drained it into his mouth.

Kristen swallowed hers cautiously. Hedda led them to her bed. The two of them lay side by side. "Close your eyes and take a deep breath." Ty felt Kristen's hand creep into his. He gave her a reassuring squeeze. "Relax your head. Feel the tension slowly drain out of your eyes, your neck, and your shoulders. Relax your chest and your stomach. Breathe freely. Relax your hips, your knees, and your ankles. Feel the tension in your feet slowly release." Hedda's voice was soothing and melodic. Ty and Kristen could feel themselves relaxing. The tea was absorbing quickly into their otherwise empty stomachs. "Picture Cali in your mind. Picture the way her voice sounds. Remember the way she would smile. Allow yourselves to only focus on her."

The darkness of their minds rippled into clarity. Cali was there laughing. Ty tried to reach out to her, but she was always just out of reach. "Cali!" His voice sounded muffled, even though he could hear her just fine.

"I don't think she can hear us." Kristen was standing beside him. Her hand was still tucked inside of his. They looked at one another taking in the fact that they were sharing a dream.

"Do I have to?" Cali slumped her shoulders and pouted. "I hate going to that place."

A voice that sounded familiar to them answered her, "Yes. You have to go. It's a tradition." Ty couldn't quite place it, and the face of the person answering was hidden behind a shadow.

Cali cocked her head to the side, "Well, if we go, can we at least get pizza later?"

The shadow laughed, "Sure we can."

Looping her hair up into a ponytail, Cali skipped off. The world around Ty and Kristen shifted and lurched. They were somewhere dark now. Candles flickered. There was a roaring sound. Thunder? No. Waves. The room was carved out of rock. Water dripped down the back of the cave and wove its way through tiny rivulets towards the lagoon.

It took a moment for their eyes to adjust, even in their dreams. Several young women in bathing suits were sitting on the floor of the cave. Older women lined the edge of the cave, giving the girls plenty of room. The shadow from before carried a jug of salt water. She poured a small amount of water in front of the first girl. The water diverted itself along the ground of the cave as if avoiding the girl. The shadow moved to the second girl. She poured more water in front of this girl. This time, the water ran to the girl and pooled at her knees. Cali had been third in line. She breathed a sigh of relief. The second girl slumped lower, despite being congratulated by the older women in the cave.

The scene shifted again. The second girl was whispering in hushed tones to Cali. They were both dressed now, sitting on a patch of grass somewhere. "I can't do it."

"You don't have much of a choice, Summer. You were chosen."

"I overheard some of the girls talking. They said that every time this happens it is always a virgin that is picked. The only reason Denise got skipped over is because she and Bobby Turner made it all the way last summer."

"You can't change it, now though." Cali's eyes were full of sadness.

"What if I can?"

"What?"

"What if I can change it? I'm going to go see Luke tonight."

"Summer, you can't." Cali put her hand on the other girl's arm in a gesture of comfort.

"Yes, I can. I don't want this!" Tears started to well up in Summer's eyes. She pulled away from Cali and stood up. Summer turned and ran away from Cali. As Cali stood up to call after her, the scenery shifted again.

They were back in the cave now. Summer had welts on her back that looked like belt marks. "She has shamed us, and is no longer worthy to be chosen. We must choose again." The shadowy figure with the pitcher looked at the girls before her. She poured the water in front of the first girl this time. The water diverted. She poured in front of the next girl. The water diverted. Cali was next. The figure poured the water again. It pooled in front of Cali. Cali's eyes widened as she realized what had happened. She looked from Summer who was sobbing on the ground to the woman with the pitcher.

Ty let go of Kristen's hand. He tried to run towards Cali, to hold her. Almost as soon as his hand let go, his eyes opened back in Hedda's hut. He looked at Kristen. She was still asleep beside him.

"It will be harder for her to wake up, without you." Hedda eyed him.

"Why? Why will it be harder for her now?"

"It is easier to remember you are in a dream when someone else is dreaming with you. When you are alone, the reality can shift more. It can swallow you whole. That is why most people do not realize when they are in a dream. They are more open to suggestions."

Kristen's eyes moved rapidly back and forth against her eyelids. Her fingers twitched and jerked as if trying to find something solid to hold on to. The rise and fall of her breathing sped up. Her lips trembled. Senseless words tumbled out of her mouth.

"Wake her up." Ty sat up straight. "You need to wake her up, look at her."

Hedda waited, "She needs more time."

"Wake her up, now!" Kristen began to toss and turn more violently on the bed.

Hedda pursed her lips and then reached out to pinch Kristen. The girl bolted upright and fought to catch her breath. Her eyes darted around the room in panic, trying to remember where she was. "What happened?"

"He woke up before you did. It made it harder for you to come back."

"What did you see?" Ty remembered the fear that he had seen in Cali's eyes when the water pooled at her knees.

Kristen placed her hands on her head trying to remember what happened. The memory was fleeting like her dreams often were. "That shadowy figure locked Cali in her room. She said that they had already had one spoiled offering. They couldn't have a second." Kristen's eyes locked with Ty's, "The shadow disappeared after you left. I thought I recognized the voice, but I couldn't be sure until the shadow was gone. It was her mom, Ty. Her mom was involved in whatever kind of ritual thing that was."

"I never met her mom." Ty's voice was quiet. He had heard her in the background on phone calls, but he had never actually seen her.

"That would make sense then. The shared dream was a compilation of both of your realities. Since you had never seen her, it clouded her appearance. Once you were gone, Kristen's perceptions took over and filled in the blanks." Hedda handed them each a bottle of water. "This should help. What kind of rituals did you see?"

"We were in some kind of cave. There were candles and the shadow person—Cali's mom—poured some water in front of these teenage girls." Ty squinted, trying to remember while Kristen drank her water. "I think it was like the water chose them. It was almost like it rerouted its way around some of the girls until it found one that it liked. It sounds stupid when I say it out loud." He hung his head.

"Ty, we just shared a freaking dream. I think we are way passed the weird things sounding stupid phase." Kristen tipped the bottle to her lips again. Beads of sweat began to form on her forehead.

Hedda handed her a small trash can, "Here."

Kristen knitted her eyebrows together, "What is this for?" As soon as she said it, her face paled. Her stomach squeezed and seized. Her body rejected whatever tea was still in her tummy as she heaved over the trash can. "I don't feel so good."

"No, you won't for a while. It should pass in a few hours." Hedda dipped a cloth in cool water and held it up to Kristen's forehead.

The girl groaned and slipped back against the wall. "Next time, I get to wake up first."

"Hopefully there won't be a next time." Ty crinkled the sides of his water bottle.

"The next step will be a little more dangerous to try." Hedda checked the pulse in Kristen's wrist.

"What's the next step?" Ty tapped his foot anxiously on the floor. They were so close to knowing what had happened.

"The next step is a near death experience."

"What? No. No way." Kristen's words were slurred. She looked as if she could throw up again at the slightest provocation.

Ty thought for a moment, "Okay."

"What?!" Kristen tried to sit up again, but Hedda made her lean back. "You can't be serious."

"You were right when you said that Cali wouldn't have given up on us if the situation was reversed." His eyes were hard and determined. "I need closure. I need to know."

"You need to be aware that there is a possibility that I may not be able to bring you back. As with anything like this, there is a level of danger."

"I understand." He let out a long breath, "So, how do we do this?"

"The easiest way I have found has been by drowning the person. Once you are out, you will only have a few moments. It may feel longer in your mind, but I will only have six minutes to resuscitate you before brain damage starts to occur. I will begin at the three-minute mark to make sure you are back before that time."

"Ty, I don't like this." Kristen's voice pleaded with him.

"Hey, if something happens, you can just visit me in your dreams, okay?"

"Don't say stuff like that! You're going to jinx it." She frowned at him.

Ty reached over and gave her hand a squeeze, "I'll be ok. Besides, you'll be here watching over me, right."

She nodded solemnly, "Yeah."

"How many times have you done this?" Ty switched his focus to Hedda.

"Four or five times over the years. Mostly it is for spouses who just want a final chance to say goodbye."

"How many of those were successful in coming back?"

"Three. To be fair though, the ones who didn't make it back chose to stay. They couldn't bear the thought of separating again."

Kristen whimpered from the bed. Ty took a deep breath, "Okay. Let's do this."

Hedda filled a large basin with water. Ty tried to prepare himself mentally for what was coming, but how can someone really prepare themselves to drown? When she placed the basin in front of him, he gazed at himself in the reflective surface. "Whenever you're ready, we can begin."

"How do I find her?"

"Just picture her in your mind like you have been doing. I can tell you had a strong connection with her. Your threads are all intertwined." A sad smile curved the tips of Hedda's lips.

Ty nodded, "I'm ready."

Instinctually, he held his breath. Bubbles escaped his mouth as he released the air from his lungs. His body ached for more air, but he struggled to keep himself down. All sound was muffled around him.

The water distorted the noise from outside the basin. His mind began to panic. Ty had to struggle to keep Cali fixed firmly in his mind's eye. The world around his eyes darkened. Water surged in to fill his gasping lungs. His body screamed at him to tell him this was wrong. He was breathing wrong. At one point, he almost lifted his head out of the water, but Hedda held him firmly under. The world dimmed and quieted and was no more.

Ty's eyes opened. It was sunset. He couldn't see Cali, but he could sense her. She was close by. Suddenly he saw her run out of a cave farther down the beach. She was running towards him. Her legs were pumping. Sand gave way under her feet. She stumbled and started to fall. A woman glistening with water followed her. She seemed to glide across the sand leaving behind wet footprints. Around her head was a dripping circlet of seaweed. The waves longed to touch her. The surged towards her with every step she took.

Cali was getting close to the log now. The woman was gaining on her. There was no way she could outrun what was about to happen. Cali threw up her arms to shield her face and screamed. He could hear it now. He could hear the fear vibrate in the air. The woman caught Cali in her arms and stepped into the lagoon. The water seemed to swell around them and suddenly, the woman melted into the waves. Cali was drug down beneath the surface. Small air bubbles rose to the surface, and then she was washed ashore. The circlet washed up beside her.

This was how they found her. This was how Cali had been discovered. Ty sank to his knees. This was how she had died? His heart ached. He clutched at his chest. She had been so afraid. No one was here for her. Hot tears started fall into the sand.

"Hello, Ty." Cali's voice made his head jerk up. The sand was clean now with no marks of her running or of the seaweed.

"Cali?" He wanted to touch her, but he was afraid that it would shatter the vision before him.

"I missed you, too." Her sweet smile was exactly the way he remembered it. She reached out her hand and touched his cheek.

He leaned into her palm, "What happened? What was that?"

"That was Salacia, the Roman goddess of the sea. She keeps it sunny and calm here as long as she receives proper tributes." Cali knelt down beside him.

"Your mom, she...she *let* this happen to you?"

"My family is one of the oldest followers from here. It was my time."

Ty shook his head, "No! No, it wasn't your time. It was supposed to be Summer's time, but she had to go—" Cali cut him off with a kiss.

"Ty, we don't have much time. Please don't waste it on being angry. Anger won't change what happened. I don't want that to be our last memories of one another."

He wrapped his arms around her and pulled her in. He could still smell the tanning lotion on her skin, "You feel so real."

Cali laughed, "I am real, right now. Ty, you have to promise me that you won't spend your time trying to find me again after this. You still have such a wonderful life ahead of you. You can't spend it looking over your shoulder for me."

A knot formed in his throat, "I love you." His heart pounded fiercely against his chest. "I never told you that when you were..." His voice trailed off.

A single tear rolled down her cheek as she smiled, "I love you, too."

Faintly, Ty could hear someone yelling his name, "I don't know how to deal with this, Cali. How am I supposed to get over you? It's not like we just broke up. You're gone."

"They're calling for you, Ty. Our time is almost up. You need to go back." She rested her forehead against his.

"I don't want to leave you. I don't want to go back. I can stay. We can be together here."

Cali shook her head no and kissed him one more time, "No, Ty. It's not your time yet. Stand up." She pulled him up by his hands. "Are you ready?" She squeezed his hand, "Come on, Ty!" She ran towards the waves. Her blonde hair streamed behind her like a golden flag. Her heels kicked up sand like they always did when he chased her. "I'm going to win!" She laughed and looked her shoulder at him. Her blue eyes sparkled as the waves surged around her knees, "I'll be waiting for you when it's time."

Ty ran after her. When the cold water seized his lungs, he sputtered and sucked in air. His eyes opened. He was back in Hedda's hut. Coughing, he choked up water and struggled to catch his breath. He broke down and started to cry. She was gone for good this time. Kristen was kneeling beside him while Hedda patted his back to make sure he coughed up as much of the water from his lungs as he could. Sobs and coughs wracked his body.

"Did you see her?" Kristen's voice was full of terrified hope.

Ty nodded, "She's ok. She seemed happy, like she was when she was alive."

"I want to go. I want to see her again." Kristen was still weak from the dream emersion, but she struggled to make herself sound as adamant as possible.

"I don't think you can." Ty looked at Hedda for confirmation.

Hedda nodded solemnly, "Her threads are gone. She has moved on."

Kristen latched onto Ty, and the two of them held one another in a comfort embrace. Ty looked at Hedda over Kristen's head, "Thank you."

"You're welcome." Hedda smiled sadly at them. "Please don't go telling the kids at school about this. I don't want a child endangerment investigation or thirty grieving children showing up trying to contact their dead goldfish."

For some reason, her words made him chuckle. Ty realized that for the first time since Cali's death, he felt as if a huge burden had been lifted off of his chest. He could still perfectly remember her kiss and the way her lips and smiled when she said she loved him. The memories were bitter sweet, but he finally felt as though he had at least some sort of closure. It was no wonder some people chose to stay dead. When someone is grieving so hard for a loved one they have lost, that they try to use a near death experience to contact them, it is hard to come back from that. Just seeing her made him want to stay there. He didn't care about the ones he would be leaving behind or the future he would be giving up. A decision like that doesn't just end one person's suffering. It passes it along to all of the people that are left behind. Even in death, Cali was watching out for him, making the tough decisions.

Ty and Kristen left Hedda's hut and walked down to the ocean. "You know," Kristen leaned her head against her friend's shoulder, "the lagoon always made me think of her, even before her death."

"It's hard to imagine the beach without her footprints in the sand, or the waves without her hair bobbing on the surface."

"Do you really think she's ok now?" Kristen's voice broke as she talked.

"Yes. I really do." He looped his arm around her shoulder lazily.

"I wish I could have said goodbye to her."

Ty squeezed her, "She knows we care about her."

"What are we going to do about her mom and that crazy cult thing?"

"Honestly, I think it would be pretty hard for us to prove anything. What are we going to do, go tell the police a dead girl showed us a sacrificial ritual while we were passed out after drinking some weird tea that the voodoo woman gave us?"

"We can't just do nothing."

"Maybe we can't by ourselves, but if we got Summer and some of the other girls involved, we might be able to wreck their alter or something. If we can't stop the generation that is in charge, we can stop the one that will inherit it."

"Do you think there will be any backlash from that?"

Ty widened his stance, "Cali said the goddess was for sunlight and calm waters. I think I'm ok with some choppy waves if the local girls get to stay alive."

"Bring on the rain."

Determination settled in both of their eyes. They stood their looking at the water the glistened in the light. How could something so beautiful hide a secret that was so dark? In the distance against the horizon, thunder crackled across the sky. Lightening licked its forked tongue across the clouds. The water ebbed from the shore, and a cool breeze blew through their hair. Ty breathed in the fresh air, heavy with the threat of rain and storms. It was as if the water knew of their intentions to stop the sacrifices, and after what they had witnessed in the past few days, they couldn't write it off as entirely impossible. Ty's bangs swirled around his eyes, and the sand began to skim across the surface of the beach. The water darkened to reflect the sky. He could sense it in every part of him now: the tides were changing.

IN WITH A BAD CROWD

Michael S. Roberts

CHAPTER ONE

Jesse James Hewitt never knew when the killings would come.

All he knew was that violence was the only tool he had.

He wasn't like other serial killers who stalked their victims and preplanned their attacks. Jesse's victims were random, in all shapes, sizes and colors.

That is how he stayed under the radar.

But his hair trigger temper could go off at any time. Right now, as he parked the stolen Toyota Camry in front of the corner grocery store, he felt happy. He had a little money in his pocket and for the next week had a place to stay at his uncle's pad.

Jesse James did, in fact, look like a modern Jesse James. He wore flared out jeans with a leather vest over a blue denim shirt. He ditched the skin head look years ago and instead grew his hair out long, a tousled mop of brown curls that he rarely combed. He had ice blue eyes that charmed many a woman until they got to know the man behind the eyes and soon felt repulsed.

Jesse walked into the store and noticed the young Asian kid leafing through the latest X-men in front of the comic rack.

He approached the young man, startling him as he craned his neck to look at his comic book cover.

"Wolverine and Kitty Pryde!" Jesse said. "Yeah, I'd fuck her."

Walking through the store, Jesse whistled in tune with the Taylor Swift swing that played on the overhead radio. Bored, he picked up a loaf of Wonderbread off the shelf then tossed it aside. Heading toward the beverage aisle, he reached inside the glass and picked up a bottle of his favorite drink.

Chocolate Yoo-Hoo.

He ripped off the lid and guzzled the contents down, the chocolate milk dripping off the side of his mouth.

Belching loud, he drifted over to the second of the three store aisles, grabbing a box of chocolate donuts. His thick fingers ripped through the plastic, breaking off a piece of a donut.

Jesse looked out at the store front window as a police car sped down the street, sirens blaring. Another squad car followed, then another.

"Uh oh," Jesse cried out. "The natives are restless."

Jesse tossed a chunk of the chocolate donut into his mouth before placing the box on the cashier's counter. An Ethiopian girl, no more than twenty years old, gave him a courtesy smile which quickly disappeared. She had caramel-colored skin and had dyed her hair blonde, leaving the tips dark brown. Her name tag read 'Naomi'.

"Hi," Jesse said.

"You find everything okay?" she asked.

"Definitely," he said, eyeballing the slim young woman up and down. "Anybody ever tell you that you look like Jessica Alba?"

"Who?"

"You know, the actress. Full lips. Beautiful face. If she were black, you'd look just like her. Or maybe she'd look just like you."

"I don't know who you're talking about," Naomi said.

"That's charming," he said. "Where are you from?"

"Ethiopia."

"I would have guessed Eritrea," he said, guzzling down the Yoo-Hoo.

"I need to scan it," she said, holding her hand out.

"Oh right," he said, handing the bottle to the young woman.

"Do you like your job?"

"Will this be all, sir?" Naomi asked, ignoring his question.

"No," Jesse said. "You're a beautiful girl and I'm really interested in how you got here and where you're going. What time do you get off?"

"When do I get off?"

"As often as you can, right?" Jesse laughed loud.

Naomi rolled her eyes.

He looked back at the storefront window. "Open twenty-four seven. How about you? Are you open twenty-four seven?"

"Is this your best game?"

"You couldn't handle my game with a referee and a whistle."

Naomi punched buttons on the cash register. "That will be five dollars."

"Think about it," he said. "You. Me. A glass of scotch in front of a warm fire."

"I don't think so."

"Can you look me in the eye when you say that?"

Naomi complied with his request, her facial expression annoyed. "I'll say this real slow so that you can understand. I. Don't. Think. So."

"I have to take you out," Jesse said. "Sometimes, you meet a person and you just know, do you know what I mean, baby?"

"Five dollars, asshole."

"Asshole," Jesse said, his eyes flickering from lust to hatred. "Is that what I am?"

"Sometimes you meet a person and you just know, do you know what I mean?"

"I just hate it," Jesse said, pulling out his gun. "When people come to this country."

He fired into the girl's stomach.

"And they don't see that I'm a local boy that made good."

Jesse grabbed his box of donuts and headed out of the store, leaving Naomi writhing in pain on the floor. The Asian boy dropped the comic and cowered in fear.

Jesse sneered at the young man then feinted as if he were about to shoot him.

"Boo!"

The Asian kid bolted out of the store, running across the street and into traffic. Horns blared.

"Run!" Jesse laughed, blowing the coils of smoke away from his gun. "Run, China Boy, Run!"

CHAPTER TWO

Kelly had walked up and down the liquor aisle for over a half-hour now. Usually, there would be someone in his face asking if he needed help. But this storekeeper seemed content to watch the television up on the corner wall. An obese woman with tinted eyeglasses she stared up at the television screen oblivious to her surroundings.

Kelly knew the feeling. He felt like everything around him was television and that he was an uncredited player in the script. His emotions felt as if they were trapped in quicksand, his tumultuous childhood traumatizing his brain into an endless loop of bad memories.

A permanent nightmare.

Kelly thought he looked inconspicuous. He wore a Golden State Warriors baseball cap and a long black trench coat two sizes too big. Wire-rimmed glasses covered his face which he always kept downcast, giving him the look of a schoolyard pervert. Underweight and undersized, Kelly cultivated the creepy look. It kept people away from him.

"I can't do it," he muttered. "I can't fucking do it."

He went up and down the aisle again but this time he grabbed the bottle of 'two buck Chuck' and hid it inside his trench coat.

"You can do it," he hissed. "Just fucking do it."

He turned down the aisle again.

"No, I can't," Kelly placed the bottle back on the shelf.

"What the fuck are you doing?" Jesse asked, blocking the path of the young man.

"Excuse me?"

"You don't want the booze?"

"No, sir."

"What's wrong with it."

"I'm trying to give it up."

"Everybody's trying to give something up," Jesse said, taking the bottle of Two Buck Chuck back off the shelf. "That's why everybody is so damn miserable. You gotta do the things you love!"

Kelly looked over at the cashier who sat oblivious to their conversation. He saw that her name tag read 'Rosie'.

"See this?" Jesse asked, holding up the bottle of Chocolate Yoo-hoo. "My dentist says I have to stop drinking these. Causes a bunch of cavities. And heart disease. But I can't stop myself. Tastes too damn good. Want to try?"

Kelly shook his head.

Jesse took another swig of his chocolate then eyeballed the wine bottle. "2014. Vintage! You like the old stuff?"

"Yes, sir."

Jesse popped open the cork. "Here," he said, extending the bottle to Kelly. "Try it."

Kelly looked away, a nervous tic in his neck.

"What's wrong? Cat got your tongue?"

"No, sir."

"You got issues," Jesse said, watching Kelly twitch as he started to back down the aisle.

"What's wrong now?" Jesse asked.

Kelly backed into a Mexican woman with a cart full of six packs. She looked to be nine months pregnant.

"Damn, *mamacita*," Jesse said as the woman walked by. "Way to start the kid off right."

"*Chinga tu madre*," the woman said.

"*Adios, amiga*," Jesse rolled his eyes, walking toward Kelly. "You see, that is what I'm talking about. Poor kid has a mother that is boozing it up and he isn't even out of the womb yet. He's got no chance, that kid. Starting off life behind the eight-ball with a mother like that, right?"

Kelly nodded his head in agreement.

"Come on," Jesse said, motioning Kelly to follow him. "You're a cool dude. Good listener. Sometimes you look at somebody and you just know, you know what I mean?"

The two stepped over to the cashier who never took her eye off the television. A game of Jeopardy was on.

Jesse handed the woman a $20 bill for the $15 bottle.

"Here you are, ma'am," he said. "Keep the change."

The cashier rolled her eyes.

"I think you and I are on the same frequency," Jesse said, leading Kelly out of the store. "Are you from the Bay Area?"

"No sir," Kelly said.

"Well, we don't have that in common. But that's okay."

He handed the bottle of wine to Kelly. "Are there houses of ill-repute where you're from?"

"What's that?"

"No worries, buddy, no worries," Jesse said. "I'm going to show you the time of your damn life. Gonna be like two sailors out on leave. That's right. That's just what we're going to do."

The cashier turned her head away from the television as a news report came on.

The reporter talked about a serial killer on the loose. White male, black baseball cap and glasses.

Rosie paid no mind to the broadcast, she walked to the front door and flipped over the closed sign.

The West Oakland sky had darkened, leaving blood orange hues of pollution on the horizon.

"Look at this shit," Jesse said as they walked down the street outside the liquor store. He shook his head as he gazed upon the abandoned storefronts and houses covered in graffiti. "Street art, my ass. Bunch of crap. Broken windows. Broken condoms. Broken lives. The fuck is wrong with these people?"

Kelly looked unnerved as the light in front of them turned red.

"Come on," Jesse said, crossing against the light. "What are you a Boy Scout?"

Kelly squinted as he looked up at the red light.

"Let's go, dude."

The light turned green and he continued to follow Jesse, not knowing why.

"Where you parked?" Jesse asked.

"I don't have a car."

"You walked? This is a dangerous place for a white boy. I mean we can walk down the streets here in Oakland and nothing will happen to us. Maybe. But absence of evidence isn't evidence of absence. We walk around here long enough someone will try and rob us. That's why we have to stick together. Can't be walking around alone, just one white boy against ten of them-"

"I take the bus," Kelly said. "I have a disability."

"Disability? What kind?"

"Mental."

"Like, you see psychiatrists and shit?"

"Yes, sir."

"Are you crazy?"

"No, sir. I just see and dream about things. And I do things. Sometimes I can't remember if it was real or a dream."

"But you do see a psychiatrist?"

"Yes, sir."

"They worth the money?"

"County pays for it. Plus I get a free bus pass."

"Right on," Jesse said. "Hey, if everyone else in this city gets freebies so can we. People around here are so ugly they make my eyes hurt. They can give them all the welfare they want as long as I don't have to see them. Man, if I were president I would change things, that's for shit-sure. I would test out bio-weapons here. You know, chemicals and shit. Release it into the atmosphere, turn these assholes into mutants. Kinda like the Island of Dr. Moreau. It would be awesome."

"Yes, sir."

"Well, will you look at that."

The two stop in front of a parked Mercedes. Jesse pointed at the bumper sticker that read "Co-Exist" and "Peace."

"See that's what I'm talking about," Jesse said. "Can you believe this shit? Perfectly good German car and they put all that shit on there. Co-exist? Muslims are taking over our damn country and we got assholes with bumper stickers promoting-"

Working himself into a fury, Jesse kicked in the rear brake light before finishing his sentence.

The car alarm went off and startled Kelly.

"Teee haaaawww!" Jesse said, smashing in the other brake light. "Come on!"

Kelly followed Jesse as they ran over to a dilapidated Toyota Camry across the street. The license plate read BAD AZZ.

"This is me," Jesse said, walking to the passenger side door and unlocking it. "Saw the license plate and just had to have it."

"I can't go with you, sir."

"Why not? I think you're cool."

"I don't know you, sir."

"I ain't a fag. Do you think I'm a fag?"

"No, sir."

"Well, let's do this," Jesse reached into his back holster and took out his gun, taking the clip out and then shoving it back in. "Now get in the fuckin' car and let's get rowdy like good sailors should."

Kelly nodded and got into the vehicle.

"Nice to see you changed your mind," Jesse said, hiding the gun in his back pocket again. "Only fools and the dead never changed their mind."

CHAPTER THREE

Jesse drove down the street like a maniac, alternately speeding up then slowing down. He swerved in front of cars, flipping the bird indiscriminately.

Kelly stared straight ahead looking scared shitless.

"Look man, I didn't mean to pull the gun on you," Jesse said. "I promised you a good time, right? We gonna get some whores. Show you what a cool guy I am. How's that sound?"

Kelly shrugged his shoulders.

"The Warriors ain't playing tonight," Jesse pointed at Kelly's baseball cap. "You watch the game last night?"

"No."

"Me neither," Jesse said. "Shit, why do that when you can go out and get some poontang, you know what I mean?"

Jesse looked out the side window and saw a blonde woman walking down the street. Dressed in business attire, her suit did little to conceal her figure.

"Holy shit!" Jesse slowed the vehicle down. "Curves for days!"

The woman turned her head and looked at the men staring at her.

"Hey darlin'" Jesse said.

Rolling her eyes, the woman turned around and began walking in the opposite direction.

"Well, fuck you then," Jesse laughed. "We could have you cumming instead of going, ain't that right, friend?"

Looking up ahead, Jesse saw a brunette walking, her eyes focused on her cell phone.

"Hot, hot, hot," Jesse said. "All these young Cal students out here sometimes. Usually trying to score some dope. What is your type? Me? I don't really have a type. I like them all really. Tall, short. Big ass. Little ass. I just like pulling girls hair. That's what gets me off. It's primal, you know. Doggy style."

They slow down and see a prostitute up ahead. She's blonde, very tall and leaning up against the pole of a bus stop.

Upon seeing Jesse's car slowing down, she twirled around the pole, like a stripper.

"Here we go," Jesse lowered his voice. "Think we might have a live one here."

Jesse stopped the vehicle next to the woman who poked her head in on the passenger side.

"Hey boys, you need a date?"

Her face had pock-marks, as if she had small-pox. Her half-lidded jaundice eyes a dead giveaway of her crack whore status.

Jesse slammed on the gas. "Good God! Did you see that? I've seen ugly but goddamn! And she had no teeth! Then again she doesn't need teeth for what she does!"

Jesse looked over at Kelly and noticed him staring at a different brunette up ahead. The girl stood with her arms crossed, emphasizing her ample cleavage.

"There you go," Jesse said. "There you go."

He stopped the car in front of the woman.

Upon closer inspection, her hair was dark blonde with brown streaks. A light skinned Latina, with full lips and green eyes. In her mid-twenties, she smiled wide as Jesse drove up.

"Two good looking guys in here. How's it going?"

"Will you do the things she won't?" Jesse asked.

"I'm the girl your mami and your papi warned you about," she said. Her voice breathy, with an accented lilt, like a breeze combing through dry leaves on a hot summer night.

"What's good on the menu?"

"That depends on how hungry you boys are," the woman said, reaching down and grabbing Kelly's crotch on 'hungry.'

Kelly shuddered in fear.

"My friend over here is starving," Jesse laughed. "As in he has not had a meal in years, if you catch my drift."

"Well, there will be plenty on the plate for both of you."

"Hop in, *mamacita*," Jesse said.

Kelly watched as the woman got into the car. His heart began to pound and his throat began to feel parched, her sweet perfume quickly filling the vehicle.

Reminding him of his mother.

CHAPTER FOUR

"My name is Maricela," she said from the backseat, looking over at Kelly on the passenger side.

Kelly said nothing, holding the wine bottle to his chest and pursing his lips.

"Is he mute?" Maricela asked Jesse. "Or deaf?"

"He doesn't open up until he really trusts someone," Jesse said. "He's smart that way. Do you always judge people?"

"I'm not judging," Maricela said. "Just asked him a damn question."

"Now you're trying to make him feel bad," Jesse said. "You're supposed to make us feel good. Make me and him feel like kings. Right, Kelly?"

Jesse reached over and playfully hit Kelly in the arm.

"I'll do that and more," Maricela said.

"Damn skippy," Jesse said. "Tee haaawww!"

"You're not high are you?" she asked.

"I'm high on life," Jesse said. "Hangin' with my homie here and about to bust a nut on a fine ass Latina."

"Well, thank you, handsome."

"Here," Jesse reached over and took the wine bottle out of Kelly's hand. "Let's get this party started."

Kelly grabbed the wine back, agitated.

"I didn't mean what I said," Maricela said to Kelly, running her fingers through the hair underneath his cap. "You seem nice. And cute. Sometimes you just know, you know what I mean? You look at someone and you get a feeling about them. It is a survival trait among us escorts."

Kelly pulled back then gave in to the woman's touch.

"There you go," Jesse said. "My friend here is an introvert. Just takes some time before he opens up to you."

"I've seen it all, dude, believe me," Maricela said. "There was this guy the other night who wanted me to shave off his chest hair. And there was this other dude that wanted me to take out this dildo he had shoved up his ass. When I took it out, the dildo was still vibrating."

"Sick fucker," Jesse said. "What a sick fuck."

"Can you imagine shoving a dildo up your ass and than calling an escort to fish it out?" Maricela asked.

"My imagination can't go that far," Jesse said.

"Maybe he called one escort to put it in and then called another to take it out?" Kelly asked.

"There you go," Jesse said. "See? He needs to get to know you before he talks."

"There's my place," Kelly said, pointing in the distance.

The television was already on when the trio stepped inside. A news reporter held up a bottle of Charles Shaw wine, explaining how forensics determined the amount of poison that a serial killer used to murder his victims.

"Nice!" Jesse said as he entered Kelly's house. Faded flowered prints marked the wallpaper but Kelly had no pictures or paintings, only one mirror in the center of the living room.

Maricela walked over to the mirror, dabbing her make-up and adjusting her cleavage.

"This is a nice place, friend," Jesse said. "I can spend lots of time up in here. We can watch TV, play video games, shoot the shit. Do you have an X-Box? My kind of place here."

Kelly said nothing as he entered the kitchen and set the wine bottle down, half-listening as Jesse continued to jabber on.

On the counter, he saw the rat poison and weed killer boxes next to the wine bottle. He quickly grasped the incriminating evidence and shoved them into his trench coat.

"Not a bad view," Jesse said, opening than closing the window curtain. "This place is what blue collar is supposed to look like. Nothing fancy. Just warm coziness. This is America! Shit man, we should go out and get an apple pie to go with that wine."

"You sound like a politician," Maricela said.

"I am the King," Jesse said. "A king. Have you ever been to L.A.?

"Yeah, I go down south sometimes."

"I was there last month. Hollywood. What a bunch of freaks! I went there thinking I could get away from all these Occupy Idiots and what happens? I get caught up in their protest! Wanted to shoot every one of those tree-hugging bitches!"

Kelly placed the poison inside a cabinet and tried to step back out of the kitchen when Jesse stepped in front of him.

"Freakin' idiots!" Jesse screamed in Kelly's face. "Do you know what I mean? These fuckers should go out and get a damn job. Am I right?"

"Right," Kelly nodded his head.

"That's right, buddy," Jesse said, sidestepping Kelly and entering the kitchen. "What kind of grub you got, man?"

Jesse ignored the ant trail on the counter and opened the refrigerator. "What kind of goodies do we have going on in here?"

Kelly crossed and uncrossed his arms, looking nervous.

"Nice!" Jesse said. "Hey man, there is only one ice cream flavor in the world. Only one. Care to guess?"

Kelly shook his head.

Jesse took out an ice cream carton from the freezer in triumph. "Vanilla! Damn, we have a lot in common."

Jesse opened up one of the drawers and grabbed a spoon.

"Come on," Jesse said. "Let's get the party started."

The two walked back into the living room.

Maricela has her shirt off, standing there wearing nothing but a black bra and jeans.

"Wow," Jesse said.

"You like?"

"Nice artwork," Jesse's eyes scanned up and down Maricela's tattooed body. A snake went down her left arm and she had pentagrams on both shoulders. "You're a devil woman."

"I got into the occult in college," Maricela said, looking down at her own tattoos. "Did a mid-term paper on this occult in Mexico then I got interested in the stuff. This one here is the eye of horus."

Maricela pointed down at her belly-button, the Egyptian symbol of protection inked on her stomach.

"So gentleman," she said. "Are we going one at a time or is this a threesome?"

"My friend here goes first," Jesse said, scooping out a spoonful of the ice cream and letting holding it out to Maricela. "Let's make it special."

Maricela wrapped her lips around the spoon, sucking off the ice cream as she sat down on the chair behind her.

"No," Kelly squealed.

Maricela sprang out of the seat.

"Not that chair!" he yelled.

Maricela stepped away from the chair and gave Jesse a startled look. "Are you sure he's alright?"

"I said don't judge him," Jesse said before taking a few steps back with the young man. "You hearing voices?"

"Loud and clear," Kelly said.

"Alright now," Jesse said. "That's nothing to be ashamed of. You should be proud of that. Been hearing voices all your life and you're still here. You're a damn soldier."

"I am?"

"Hell fucking yeah," Jesse said. "But she'll help you get rid of those voices, okay?"

Jesse patted Kelly on the back before heading into the kitchen.

"Relax, dude," Maricela whispered.

Kelly slowly turned his back to the young woman but she spun him around gently.

"It is really easy," Maricela said, taking Kelly by the hand. "First timers are my specialty."

She lead him to the chair to sit down and he shuddered.

"Easy," Maricela said. "We don't have to do it there."

She placed her hands on both of his shoulders and led him over to the couch.

Kelly sat down, eyes downcast.

Maricela played with unbuckling his belt until he turned away.

"Okay, okay, we can do other things."

She let the strap of her bra fall down off her shoulder.

Kelly looked up with painful shyness, licking his cracked lips as he stared at Maricela's breasts.

"You're a titty man," she laughed. "There you go."

Maricela took his hand and placed it on her left breast, letting the young man knead away.

"Gently," she said, tilting her head back in pleasure. "Gently. There you go. You like that?"

Kelly nodded, noticing the upside down cross that Maricela had tattooed on the underside of her wrist.

"Me too, baby. Me too."

Kelly turned to the kitchen door and shuddered as he saw Jesse standing there, watching.

"What are you doing?" Jesse asked. "I said he is a beginner. He's shy with women. You gotta take it slow."

"You get off on taking a front row seat?" Maricela asked. "We were taking it slow."

"Then why is he so freaked out?"

Maricela glared at Jesse.

"Come on," Jesse said, waving her away from the couch. "Give us a minute here. Go upstairs to the bedroom and we'll be right there. We need to have a man to man."

Maricela got up off the couch, rolling her eyes as she made her way up the steps.

"This always works for me," Jesse said, waving the wine bottle in his hand as he sat down next to Kelly. "Loosens you up. Breaks down whatever blockages you got going on in your big head and little head."

Kelly gulped hard.

"We'll be right there!" Jesse called out. "Go ahead and get nekkid! He'll be right up."

CHAPTER FIVE

Maricela entered the bedroom and closed the door. The lamp on the desk illuminated the neatly made bed. There were pictures of dead bugs on the wall which gave her the creeps. She looked closer and realized that they weren't pictures at all. They were dead moths and butterflies inserted between the glass and cardboard backing.

A buck is a buck, she thought, seeing more than her share of strange. She walked over to the TV set and pushed the button to turn it on, looking for the remote control on the counter.

"Look man," Jesse said, putting his arm around Kelly like a big brother. "There is only one thing you need to know about women, okay? You have to satisfy their needs. Once you do that, you are in. Okay? So do you know what women want more than anything?"

"Help?"

"No, they want to get high," Jesse said, removing his arm around Kelly, struggling to uncork the wine bottle he held between his legs. "You just have to find out what women want. Some women you meet are going to want fun. Power. Status. Money. That is why whores like

Maricela are so great. There is no drama. You pay your fee and get what you want."

Jesse popped the cork on the bottle and Kelly shuddered. He knew he had placed the poison in that one.

Jesse raised the bottle to his lips but Kelly grabbed it out of his hands.

"No!"

Jesse stared at Kelly for a beat.

"You never got to have any fun did you?" Jesse asked.

"She used to send me to the store," Kelly said. "With a note to get booze."

"Your mom?"

Kelly nodded.

"No worries, man," Jesse said, moving closer to Kelly now. "My folks were the same way. Both of them alcoholics. Dad was a functional one. Went to work every day. Worked his ass off every day. Then one day he shot himself. Just stepped into the house and blew his brains out. Died all alone."

"I never knew my Dad. Never. No pictures. Nothing. Bet he died alone."

"My mom didn't even cry," Jesse said. "Just kept bringing men over. Fucked every one. Didn't care if I was listening or watching or what. Definitely didn't care that my Dad found out. She was evil, man. Evil incarnate."

"Mine too," Kelly whispered, hunching his back as of the ghost of his mother could hear him.

"Mine was worse than an evil step mom. She was a real mom."

Maricela laid on the bed, noodling around on her cell phone which now showed a dead battery. Looking around for an extension so she could recharge it, the screen shot on the television caught her eye.

The report showed a police sketch of a man that resembled Jesse.

"Police said to be on the lookout for the license plate BAD AZZ in a late model white or gray Toyota. If you have any information regarding the suspect please call 911 immediately."

Maricela toggled on her cell phone again. Dead.

She ran over to the bedroom door but when he opened it she saw Jesse standing outside with Kelly behind him.

"Someone is in a hurry to get started," Jesse said. "If you're that horny you can go ahead and start without us."

"Was just wondering where you guys were," she said.

"He's ready and rarin' to go," Jesse said, placing his arm around Kelly and shaking him. "Go get 'em, Tiger."

Maricela forced a smile, stepping aside to let the men in.

"You ready to show him a good time?" Jesse asked.

"But of course," she said, her voice quavered, betraying her nervousness. "Give the man a little privacy."

Maricela took Kelly by the hand and led him further into the bedroom. She attempted to close the door but Jesse stopped her.

"Nothing goes on behind closed doors around here," Jesse said.

Kelly looked back at Jesse as if he were about to go into the electric chair.

"You can do it, buddy!"

"Come on, handsome," Maricela motioned for Kelly to sit down on the bed. The young man took a deep breath, eyes downcast until he slowly looked up at woman stroking his upper thigh. "Do you think I'm pretty?" she asked.

Kelly could only nod his head, smitten by her beauty.

"Thanks," she said.

Jesse made as if he were going down the steps but stopped at the top, kneeling down so he remained out of Maricela's eyeline.

He listened to Maricela's voice, his heart beating in anticipation of what came next just like when his mother had men over at the house.

"You look like a movie star," Kelly blurted out. "Like you should be in porn or something."

"We should go someplace else," Maricela said. "Just the two of us. Okay?"

"But what about my friend? You don't like him?"

"I like you better," she said, kissing him on the lips then hugging him.

Kelly shuddered in delight.

"You have to leave," she said, nuzzling his ear. "This dude is a serial killer. Okay? He'll kill us both."

"What the hell is going on here?" Jesse asked stepping through the door, his entire body an antennae telling him that something was up.

"This young stud is pitching up a tent!" Maricela said, standing back up and pointing at Kelly's crotch.

Jesse grabbed her wrist before she could walk back downstairs. "Where are you going?"

"I have to get us some protection. Duh." Maricela hurried out of the bedroom.

Jesse sat down next to Kelly. "What did she say to you?"

"She has a crush on me."

"Ha!" Jesse laughed. "See? See what happens when you give women what they want. You gonna start listening to me now?"

They both hear Maricela's high heels running down the steps.

Jesse sprinted down the stairs and caught her just as she reached the door.

He spun her around, angry. "It ain't polite to leave a party early! Thought you were going to get some protection?"

"I left the rubbers in the car."

"Left the rubbers in the car, bullshit!" Jesse slammed her against the wall. "You're a damn devil. A thief!"

Jesse reached inside Maricela's purse and pulled out a wallet.

Kelly's wallet.

"Stop!" Kelly said, coming down the steps.

"Lifted it straight outta your pocket, dude!" Jesse threw the wallet back at Kelly.

Maricella ran over to the wine bottle on the coffee table and smashed it against the edge. Grasping the bottle by the handle, she held it in front of her as a weapon.

"Ooooh," Jesse said. "Come on, bitch! Come on, let's see what you got!"

Maricela's face contorted into that of feral woman, fighting for her life. She stabbed at Jesse, lacerating his hand with the glass.

"Bitch!" he said.

Maricela ran toward the kitchen.

Jesse gave chase until Kelly jumped on his back.

"Leave her alone!" Kelly screamed.

Jesse threw off the little man with ease, pushing him into the chair. "You crazy? This bitch just tried to rob you, man!"

Racing through the kitchen, Maricela opened the cellar door and locked it behind herself.

"Bitch!" Jesse screamed, pounding on the wood. "Bitch!"

He kicked the cellar door again and again.

"Fuck off!" Maricela cried out.

Jesse looked down at his hand, his blood dripping on the kitchen floor.

Walking back into the living room, he saw Kelly sitting on the couch watching TV, another wine bottle in his hand.

"Dude!" Jesse said, holding up his bloodied hand. "Look what your damn girlfriend did to me."

"She's not my girlfriend."

"Where's the key to your basement?" Jesse asked, taking out his gun. "Or do I have to just blow shit open?"

"I have the key," Kelly said, glaring at Jesse.

"Hey man," Jesse said. "You're looking at me with some hate in your eye. I told you that girl was a thief. A demon. You see that upside cross on her wrist? She's a devil worshiper! Doesn't Satanism freak you the fuck out? Let's go kill her ass."

"She's already dead," Kelly said, staring off into the distance, in his own world.

"All of mine are dead too," Jesse said pointing the gun at his own temple. "So let's kill another one."

"She told me she loved me."

"Of course," Jesse said. "I knew that. That's why I got her for you. Figured she was just your type."

He took the wine bottle out of Kelly's hand and guzzled it down. "Aaaaahhh!"

Kelly returned his attention to the television, his eyes transfixed.

"What is it, goddamnit?" Jesse asked, turning toward the TV. He saw the police sketch of himself and the license plate.

BAD AZZ.

Enraged, he shot a bullet through the TV.

CHAPTER SIX

Maricela heard the gunshot. Startled, she looked around the cellar for a weapon of any kind. She found a fire poker in the corner and gripped it hard.

Kelly ran back toward the cellar door with the keys in hand. "I'll get you out," he called out to Maricela. "I'll help you."

Jesse chased after him but fell down, the room spinning, his entire body sweating. He retched again, with blood streaked bile coming out of his mouth. He looked at Kelly staring at him, wild-eyed with fear. His friend went in and out of focus, doubling and distorting like a kaleidoscope.

What was in that wine?

Maricela took the fire poker and smashed out the tiny cellar windows.

"Help me!" she screamed. "I've been kidnapped! Help me!"

Kelly put the key in the cellar lock but could not get it to open.

Jesse pitched forward over the sink and retched again.

"The fuck you put into that wine?" Jesse asked, purple bile spilling out of his mouth.

"I'm sorry," Kelly said.

Falling to the ground, Jesse pointed the gun at Kelly.

"I was just trying to be a good friend," Jesse said.

Maricela screamed as she heard the gunshot.

She scrambled back up the cellar steps. Pressing her ear to the door, she waited several minutes before she unlocked it.

Opening up the door, she saw both Jesse and Kelly on the floor in a growing pool of blood.

Kelly laid on his stomach, the blood spewing forth from the fatal gunshot blast into his belly. He stared straight ahead at Jesse who laid on his back, blood and foam caked around his lips, neck and chest.

Ants began to scuttle over their bodies.

They were both locked in a death stare at each other. The pupils of their eyes like black holes eating the whites.

Their once lonely faces no longer dark but relieved.

They didn't have to die alone.

www.ingramcontent.com/pod-product-compliance
Lightning Source LLC
Chambersburg PA
CBHW020601160726